ELECTRIC LOVE

PHILIP PALIOS

In Memory of LeRoi Moore

CHAPTER ONE

JORDAN RAN LIKE THERE WAS nothing left behind him and he didn't pay attention to what lay ahead. Every ounce of his blood pumped through his heart as fast as it could beat. The uneven sidewalk snarled up as each tree approached, mother nature slowly having her way with the insidious pavement covering every inch of this city, he thought. Jordan jumped over the gaps in the concrete and gracefully pivoted off the uprooted sidewalk, using the environment to enhance his speed. He felt like he could keep going forever, without a care for what might lay ahead.

"Get back here you motherfuckin' cheat! You don't run away from me!" came a distant shout behind him. Four seconds later Jordan heard the revving engine of C.L.'s Mercedes growing louder as it approached him. Knowing he couldn't outrun the motorized collection agent, he decided to go where the car couldn't and dodged into an alley lined with dumpsters off of 10th street. As Jordan approached the end of the alleyway, continuing to run with everything he had, he suddenly felt the cold hard impact of his skull on the pavement behind him. After the initial shock wore off, he felt an aching in his chest where C.L. had knocked him down with a baseball bat.

"You stupid ass motherfucker, think you can run from me? Think this ally doesn't just open up on the next street? That's your problem Jordan, you don't think. You don't think about what will happen when you don't pay for your dust. You don't think about where you're going. Get in the fucking car and let me give you something to think about."

C.L. grabbed Jordan by the collar and dragged him to his feet, pushing him into the back seat of his idling car. Jordan didn't put up a fight and got in the car, this was not his first visit to the backseat of C.L.'s Mercedes. He knew what was coming, he knew it would be painful, but he also held onto the belief that he would make it out alive, after all that's the only way his dealer knew they would get paid. He thought he had enough leverage to keep the game alive. He really could use a cigarette.

"Now listen, Jordan Vincent Santarelli..." came a voice he had not heard before. Jordan looked to his left and saw the face of an aging man, grey hair tucked under a bowler cap, hand gripping a cane with a polished steel top. As Jordan looked into the man's eyes he saw the face of death staring him back, this man was soulless, heartless, not human. The old man was wearing a black polyester running suit with white stripes going down the sides and a cigar sat burning in the ashtray next to him.

"...You think you have us pegged. You think you can fuck with us and come out ahead? You think you're the first dusthead to come up with this strategy? Let me tell you Jordan, I've killed dozens of dustheads with your winning strategy, and the state doesn't bat an eyelash. In fact, I'm doing them a favor getting shit like you off the streets. You're useless to me if you don't pay up. You've owed me upwards of ten grand for the past two years and paid back hardly one. You think I'm going to keep waiting? No, I'm done with you Santarelli. I'm going to give you a lot less to live for and then you're going to kill yourself. But first I'm going to get paid."

"Who the fuck are you old man? You think you can intimidate me? You haven't killed so much as a fly in your life and probably are thinking about suicide yourself now that all the blue pills stopped working for you and the dustwhores just laugh when you whip out your floppy inch."

Jordan looked at the man's hands as they smoothly picked up the cigar from the ashtray and began moving toward his face.

The old man pointed the burning end of his cigar at Jordan and held it two centimeters from his nose. Then the man stared him straight in the eye with the same soulless gaze as before, unwavering, devoid of emotion, while pushing the burning tip of the cigar into Jordan's nose. Jordan yelped in agony as the old man continued to push the cigar into Jordan's face until blood began pouring out and the screams turned into cries.

"I don't give a fuck about you kid. You're just another customer who stopped paying. Now I'm going to tell you how the next three months of your life will play out. These are the final three months of your life, and if you fuck it up I will kill you on the spot."

Jordan didn't understand what was going on anymore.

The pain in his chest and his face were overwhelming, but this was all no worse than the usual collection drill except for the unfamiliar agent of death and all the talk about killing him. In the past it was just C.L. telling him to get the money or feel the pain. The old man made things different.

"You're going to get a job offer tomorrow morning, you take it and you show up to work. Bandage up your face and get the fuck out of my car you deadbeat." The old man lifted up his cane and shoved Jordan out of the car as C.L. opened the door. Jordan fell to the pavement in front of his apartment building and crawled up the steps to the entry. C.L. followed him to the door and right as he got up on his feet C.L. slammed the baseball bat into Jordan's side, knocking him back down. C.L. spit in his face and said "You stupid motherfucker better listen." then tossed a bandage in his direction and walked off.

Jordan's apartment was in an old brick building on Union Street, a red canopy draped over the entrance and cracked concrete stairs led up to the door. The buzzer by the door still worked, but all of the names were wrong. The landlord stopped updating them ten years ago. A flower pot on each side of the entrance gave strangers the false impression that this was a classy joint. The front of the canopy had white lettering with the ink fading, it read "Joshua Tree" reflecting the owner's hippy roots. Or maybe he just liked U2. The entrance door was made of steel, painted an ugly dark green with the address printed above it. Jordan pulled the key out of his pocket and opened the door. As he stood in the drab entrance, a bank of mailboxes to his right, electrical closet to his left, the stairs going up in front of him, he waited for the door to close behind him. He struggled to stand up as he became more and more dizzy, the pain did not subside. He leaned against the banister of the stairs and looked down at the steps in front of him. "FUUUUUCKKKKK!" he yelled at the top of his lungs. With that final exaltation, he fell to his knees and laid down on the stairs. His vision blurred and faded to black.

CHAPTER TWO

THE CADENCE OF THE SNARE and kick drums offered a brisk but steady pace for what was one of the most pleasurable dreams Jordan had experienced in recent memory. The pure ecstasy he felt reminded him of his days with Fiona. As the vocals kicked in and he heard the warm throaty voice of Bob Keys sing about the delight of morning birds, skipping stones and hobos, he heard the moan of a woman. As he gradually faded into consciousness, Jordan realized that it wasn't a dream, but his erect penis, or more precisely, the vagina it was sliding in and out of, providing his euphoria.

After three more thrusts he looked up to see the long dark hair of the woman on top of him bouncing off her pale white, tattooed back with the vigorous downward motion of her hips enveloping his cock and igniting all the pleasure sensors in his brain. She continued to fuck him with great intensity, almost mechanically, until he interrupted her rhythm, asking "Who are you?" his hands grasping her thighs in a weak attempt to appear actively involved in the morning activity.

A man with a video camera standing three feet away hissed at him, when Jordan glanced over, noticing the man for the first time, he saw him holding a finger to his lips. What was going on? Suddenly, Jordan felt the rush immediately preceding ejaculation and pushed the woman off of him, shouting "Here I come!" As he finished and she cleaned up, he looked at the director, and the room he found himself in. A moment of shock and dizziness required him to sit back down on the mattress he had awoken on. He looked back up at the man with the camera and asked "What the fuck is going on? Who are you? Where am I?"

"Calm down mate!" the man replied with a half-British, half-Australian accent. "You're in your own room, don't you recognize it? I'm Victor." reaching out his hand in greeting, Jordan responded and shook hands with the man who had just filmed him fucking a woman he didn't know. "We thought we would start your new job off with a bang! How do you like Victoria? She really knows how to fuck, eh?"

Fuck. Victoria. New Job. What? "Did C.L. send you?" he asked Victor.

"Who? C.L.? I don't know who that is. Your agent? The studio sent me, you're on contract for a five-day."

"What the fuck is going on? Are you paying me? Five days of what? I need some fucking dust."

Victor handed Jordan a pre-rolled joint and lit it for him. "Calm down buddy, you're acting like this is your first gig or something. How long have you been shooting?"

"I didn't sign up for this. I work at a coffee house on Pine street."

"You're Jordan Santarelli, yeah?"

"Yeah, that's my name. How did you get in my house?"

"Your neighbor let us in, said you were in a bad way last night. She wasn't sure whether you were dead or alive. We thought Victoria could figure that out in short order, and we might get some good b-reel. You're saying this is your first shoot? We didn't request a fucking amateur, guys like you are a dime a dozen and the experienced ones don't freak out. I'm calling Vinny."

CHAPTER THREE

HANNAH WAS FIFTEEN MINUTES EARLY and found the front door was locked and the lights were out. Dreaming Tree Coffee House was in one of the half-dozen new apartment buildings going up on Capitol Hill. Each building was as plain and boring as the next, they were all made cheaply and quickly in the interest of collecting exorbitant rent from ignorant young tech workers fresh off the airplane. Dreaming Tree was the real estate developer's daft stab at having a dash of culture on the premises. The lack of creativity went all the way down to the name of the building, which wasn't really a name at all, just the street address "510 Pine." However these facts didn't bother Hannah, she knew that all it took was a bit of love, time, and creativity for her to help give the coffee shop, the building and the neighborhood the sense of artistic character that everyone in it, from the developers to the residents, so deeply desired.

One month out of college, with a BFA and dreams of imminent success, Hannah was also an experienced barista. She spent all five years of her undergraduate studies working part-time at a coffee shop in the basement of the fine arts building. In her parents mind, they wasted

$125,000 training their beloved daughter for a career that didn't require a degree at all. But Hannah was resilient to their criticisms, she had gained a robust community of fellow artists, new and old, encouraging her pursuit of art. She wasn't so cloud headed to think that she wouldn't need to work a day job, at least starting out, but she knew that art was the reason God put her on this planet, and having had the academic preparation she was ready to begin a life of creating visual and written works to help inspire the world.

As she waited for the opening shift lead to arrive, Hannah stared at the brick facade of the building. Each stone was laid so perfectly, it was hard to believe any of them had ever been touched by human hands. The grid of the brickwork could be used for a variety of mathematical studies, it was as precise as graph paper. Isn't it ironic, she thought, that imperfect brick work is so much more beautiful than the precise, mathematically perfect work that stood before her?

Her shift lead was fifteen minutes late. He looked ill and smelled like sex. His inconsistent, short-cut brown hair appeared as though he had attempted to cut it himself, failed, but left it as-is. His jeans were torn, and not in the trendy, expensive way. Standing 5'11" he was less than an inch taller than she was. Skinny as a twig, he didn't appear to have an ounce of muscle or fat on his bones. The man's pale complexion, eyes that appeared to lack a soul and skinny body suggested he might be more ghost than human. He wore a blue t-shirt reading "F*cked" which seemed appropriate given his stench of sweat and semen.

"You the new girl? Ever worked a coffee shop before?" he asked.

"Yes, five years while I was in school. My name is Hannah." She hesitantly stretched out her hand in greeting.

The man walked past her, keys in hand, he bent down to unlock the door, masking a cry of pain with a hacking cough. He opened the door and slowly stood up before pushing the door open, walking in front of Hannah.

"Clean the tables, I'll get the drip going."

"You look like you need a cup yourself, are you ok?"

"Mind your business, Hannah."

"Where are the cleaning supplies?"

Suddenly the bells hanging from the front door rang loudly as a large Arab man walked in and marched up to the smelly man who had not yet identified himself. "You're fired Jordan, get out now."

Jordan shrugged, he was not particularly surprised by the announcement and walked out as if this was a regular occurrence in his life. Hannah felt a pang of sympathy, it was clear the man was struggling, but the manager knew him much better than she did, and after all he was the boss. She bowed her head slightly as Jordan exited.

"Hannah, I'm sorry your first day is off to a bad start. Do you remember me? I'm Ali, and I'll show you how to get going. We need a new opening shift lead, maybe you?"

"Of course I remember you, Ali!" she responded, Ali was the reason she took this job. He was the most kind, loving and positive person she had met in her series of coffee house interviews. Two other coffee shops had offered her jobs, and all three had the same minimum wage pay, so choosing Ali's place was an easy decision.

The tall, elderly man with short, neatly trimmed grey hair reminded her of her faculty advisor in school, holding a ceaseless positive attitude and always carrying a smile from ear to ear. Even when he had to fire someone.

"Good, now let me show you how I like to prepare the coffee."

"Ali, this place is so plain. The white walls, the square windows, you need some art in here!"

"Yes, all in good time. We need coffee in here first." He grabbed a five-pound bag of coffee beans and began filling a measuring cup. As he proceeded to show her how to prepare the coffee, Hannah went along even though she was already intimately familiar with it all.

"You see that shop across the street? What must we do to compete with them? They have decent coffee, friendly service and low prices. What can we do?" Ali asked.

Hannah responded assertively, "We give them more than good service, we start their day with a greeting filled with love. We inspire them, we give them art."

"Yes! This is why I hired you Hannah. You understand. So many kids I interview and can't offer a job to because they hide their hearts. We must open our hearts to succeed."

Hannah nodded, then pointed at a barren wall, "I can't stand these white walls. There's no love in a white wall, Ali."

The door chime rang as the first customer of the day entered the shop. He was staring down at his smartphone and wore the same blue jeans and plaid shirt uniform that seemed to identify the tech class in this city. As he approached the counter, face still pointed downward, he said "Grande non-fat latte." It was not completely clear whether he was talking to his phone or to Hannah.

"Good morning! I'll get that latte going for you." Hannah responded. Ali rang up the distracted man, who somehow managed to pay without making any eye contact.

When Hannah first began making espresso she discovered the opportunity to make art with the foam and was overjoyed to make art a part of her work. This was before she had discovered ways to make every single moment of her life artistic, and it inspired her to not quit after the first day working the college job she didn't even really want in the first place. If it wasn't for foam art she may have never stuck with it, and wouldn't have the job she has today.

Topping the down-headed man's latte with a swirling tree branch that ended in a heart, she handed the paper cup to him and said "Enjoy" as he took it from her, still absorbed with whatever was on that four inch screen in his hand.

The man exited the coffee shop after affixing a plastic lid on top of Hannah's artwork. After he exited, Hannah looked at Ali with a sigh, "What is the world coming to?"

"There is something in these phones that is incredibly important to these young people, Hannah. Don't you have one yourself? We have a lot to compete with in order to gain their attention. But I am convinced we can give them more joy, love, art and coffee than those phones can."

"Yes, I have one, but I keep it at home." Hannah responded.

CHAPTER FOUR

JORDAN STAGGERED OUT OF THE coffee shop, his former employer. Why did this happen today? He had shown up late dozens of times and Ali never appeared to mind. And to start this new…career…in the adult film industry on the same day. This could not be a coincidence, he thought. This had to be the work of C.L. or whomever that old man in the car was. That old man said he would get a new job, and that's exactly what happened. But why?

Jordan walked back to his apartment, taking his phone out of his pocket to call his dealer. This was all too overwhelming and he had gone over a day without an ounce of dust.

"Yeah, this is Jordan. I need some dust. Now. Fifteen minutes? No, I ain't got cash I just lost my job. Fuck you, you know I'm good for it."

Walking up the hill that separated the coffee shop and his home, Jordan thought about how he might find out what was going on. Then his mind shifted to his desire to get high. How was he supposed to function without dust? Ducking through a crowd of people smoking outside a church he stopped and turned around "Anyone got some dust?" he asked, pleadingly. But the smokers just looked at him, laughing and shaking their heads.

The unusual summer humidity had Jordan drenched in sweat before he was half way up the hill. Was it the humidity or the withdrawal? His bones ached. As he approached his front door he saw blood stains on the steps, perhaps his own from the night before. Who cleaned this up? Would it be cleaned up? He reached in his pocket for his keys and remembered he left them at the coffee shop. Jordan banged on the door hoping someone would let him in, but it was quiet and no one was around. Sitting down on the stoop he felt the shooting pain in his ribs from where C.L. had clubbed him. The gut-wrenching pain from the burn on his nose suddenly bubbled up, he covered his face and began crying.

Ten minutes later his phone rang. Jordan didn't recognize the phone number. He answered, "Hello?"

"Jordan, my name is Annie. I work at the agency. I meant to call you last night to let you know about the shoot with Victor and Victoria. Sorry!"

"How did you get my phone number? Who are you? What's going on? I never signed up for this."

"Hah, Santarelli you know no one signs up for this! You're on a five-day trial. If your videos get enough hits then we'll put you on a full-time contract. You should be thanking me for finding you work, hundreds of guys would give their right thumb for a full-time porn gig. You even get medical coverage with us, who else offers that?"

Jordan had never had medical insurance before. If he was sick, his solution was to get high. If that didn't work, he went to the Emergency Room. They usually kicked him out. It was only when he got so bad his neighbors had to call an ambulance that he ever saw a doctor. That had happened five times in his life. The doctors just tell him to get off the dust, as if that would solve things.

"Fuck insurance, I need to get paid."

"Jordan, you'll get paid, but we've got a garnishment on your wages that will take quite a bit out."

"From who?"

"Well, from our distribution company actually. That's kind of strange. Oh well, what can you do?"

"Quit."

"I wouldn't do that Jordan, you know how C.L. can be."

"You know C.L.? You work for him?"

"Of course I work for him, it's his studio, agency and distribution company! He runs the show here hon."

"Of course he does." Jordan hung up his phone and tossed it on the steps of the apartment building. Crossing his arms on his knees to rest his head, Jordan's mind ran wild as he closed his eyes.

This was not the life Jordan had in mind for himself, he had never been an ambitious person, he just wanted to get by. Relax, enjoy life, have fun. That was his mantra. Neither getting in drug debt nor being unemployed were fun or relaxing. The stress and anxiety over what would happen next in his predicament only made him want to escape more than ever. He would give anything for a moment of bliss, escape, nothingness. Too much of a coward to pull the plug on his own life, he simply longed for a taste of death, a moment of freedom. His flat was barren, not an ounce of dust or any other drug, not even food or a beer in the fridge — it was completely devoid of sustenance.

An image appeared in Jordan's mind, the unforgettable beauty of Fiona. Her long red locks, deep blue eyes, pale, freckled face and beaming smile. He recalled her robust bosom and perfectly formed body. No matter how hard he tried to forget her, she kept appearing in his thoughts, his dreams, his fantasies. A woman so beautiful it gave even a devote atheist the thought that they might be wrong. As Fiona's eyes stared into Jordan's, seeming to consume every thought, every heartbeat, his entire soul, her lips parted and with grave sincerity, she said "Stop."

Unable to respond, unable to say how sorry he was, how much he longed to be with her, unable to do anything but watch, Jordan realized he was dreaming. The sad realization was powerful enough to awaken him from his dream. As he returned to the world of the living, he felt the teardrops running down his cheek and falling to the pavement below. He attempted to wipe the tears away, but only spread a mixture of dirt, tears and sweat across his face. Jordan looked up and saw a dark red van with no windows pull up and park across the street. As the driver's door opened, he recognized Victor the porn director stepping out of the van. Hoping this was all just a dream, Jordan laid his head back down and closed his eyes, desperate for Victor to be gone the next time he opened them.

Victor's voice came from a few feet away. "Aye, Jordan! You ready for your first real shoot? I've brought the queen herself, Miss Q. You're in for a treat today bruv'!"

Jordan looked up and saw Victor's face clearly for the

first time. There was something not quite right about it. He had both eyes, a nose and a mouth, two ears, but it looked as if they had all been removed and re-attached in slightly different places than they had originally been found. His neck was nearly covered in tattoos and his complexion had a red tint, as if there was too much blood pumping through his veins.

Following a few feet behind Victor was a woman who appeared to be in her mid-forties, her face covered in wrinkled skin and her chest covered with two enormous breasts, clearly filled with decades old silicon implants, bouncing like suspended water balloons with each step she took. With a lit cigarette hanging from the corner of her mouth, supported by overly-plump lips, Miss Q was not attractive to Jordan in the least.

Whispering to Victor, Jordan asked "How old is that hag?"

"Oh cheer up mate, Miss Q has more AVN awards than you can imagine! You gonna let us in or do you want to film out here?"

"Fine, fine." Victor went up to the front door and remembered that he left his keys at the coffee shop. "I left my keys at work, got to go get them. Be back in thirty."

"Don't try that shit with me you little fucker. We can shoot in the van. Forgot your keys, hah."

Jordan followed Victor and Miss Q back to the van, seeing Miss Q's large and sagging ass for the first time, only further repulsed as he thought that he would be on film having sex with this woman. As Victor opened the back doors of the van, Jordan saw why there were no windows.

Mounted on each side of the van's interior were large lamps, clearly placed to illuminate the mattress and pillows that covered the entire back of the van. Between the front driver and passenger seats, a video camera was mounted facing the bed. More lights hung from the back of the driver and passenger seats. Jordan was dismayed, not because he had never seen a van like this before, but because he never desired, nor imagined himself to be inside of one. He had seen several porn flicks, even entire websites devoted to the concept of a "shaggin' wagon," but all of a sudden the videos he had used for a brief burst of relief in the past came back to haunt him as he imagined the actors who had been put in his present circumstances.

"Jump in!" encouraged Victor, as Jordan watched Miss Q crawl in and lay in the bed on her side, looking back at Jordan with a mute expression.

"It's not so bad, just get in and we'll go get your keys." Miss Q said with a wink.

Not perceiving any options, Jordan begrudgingly hopped into the back of the van. Sitting in the far corner, as far from Miss Q as possible. Victor slammed the doors behind the two and got in the driver's seat. As he started the engine, the lights surrounding the bed turned on with a loud "click." Peeking out from the passenger seat, a woman turned on the video camera.

"A'ight kids, it's showtime!" Came the unfamiliar voice of the woman in the passenger seat.

"Who is she?" asked Jordan, staring at Victor.

"Oh, Ann, she's new. Too shy to get in front of the camera. Maybe you can help us break her in."

There was no way in Jordan's mind that he could

fathom going through with any of this. He loved sex and porn, but never wanted to take part in it, especially when he was being forced to fuck an unattractive old hag and wasn't making any money for it. He looked at Miss Q, who had slipped out of her t-shirt and jean shorts to reveal a muffin-top covering her red bikini bottoms and free hanging breasts, unburdened by the restraint of a bra.

"There ain't no way man, I'm not going through with this. You expect me to fuck her? On camera? That ain't gonna happen. C.L. can go fuck himself."

"Calm down mate, you'll get used to it. Ain't a bad way to get paid you know. If you can't get it up, I've got something here that can help you out."

Victor pulled out a needle and some sort of liquid, indicating for Jordan to inject the substance into his penis. Jordan drew back.

"I ain't fuckin' this ugly old bitch in the back of your ghetto van. There's a good god damn reason I'm not aroused, and I intend to keep it that way. Forget about it."

"Look, we can go get your keys and do it at your place. How's that work for you?"

Jordan reluctantly agreed. He was desperate to postpone an intimate encounter with Miss Q and directed Victor to the coffee shop.

Miss Q didn't appear to have feelings one way or the other about what was going on, instead she just reached down and began to masturbate. Ann was not to be seen, having turned off the camera and sitting up front quiet as a mouse. Victor seemed agitated, as if he expected things to go more smoothly than this. Jordan was just glad he could keep his clothes on for now.

As the van rolled to a stop near Dreaming Tree, Victor looked back at Jordan and said "Door's unlocked. We're filming this one way or another bud, if we don't shoot today your contract is scratch."

Not wasting a beat, Jordan unlatched the back door of the van and jumped out, slamming the door shut behind him and hoping the van might just roll away and never come back. But it stayed there, idling in front of the coffee shop. As Jordan approached the shop's entrance he could see Hannah and Ali through the window, hard at work with a store full of customers. The smooth bass notes of Stephan Lessard greeted him as he entered the shop. Jordan slowly walked to the counter and saw Ali glare at him, stepping from the espresso machine to address the intruder.

"What do you want?" Ali asked.

"My keys. I left my keys here this morning."

Ali looked at Hannah with a question mark expression on his face. She nodded in affirmation and went to the back room, returning with Jordan's keys. She handed them to Ali and returned to the cash register without a word. Ali took the keys and searched through them for the store key, removing it from the loop and then handing them to Jordan. He looked deep into Jordan's eyes with the loving kindness of a grandfather to his troubled grandson, nodded and then turned away without saying a word.

As Jordan turned to leave, he saw Ann enter. "I could use a cup of coffee." she said to him in passing. Then she grabbed his forearm, bringing him to a halt and said "C.L. got you into this too?"

CHAPTER FIVE

JORDAN LOOKED AT ANN AND nodded, he wasn't entirely surprised to learn that she was roped into this gig the same way he was. When he first saw her he assumed she was just another actress like Miss Q, in it for the money. He was relieved to learn that he wasn't the only one in this predicament. Perhaps she knew more about what was going on than he did.

As the two stood frozen in passing, he asked "What do you know?"

"We must run." she said as her body spun around facing the door alongside Jordan. Ann began to run without letting go of Jordan's arm. The two exited the store and began to run down the street toward downtown. With Victor perched just outside the door it was impossible to escape his sight. As the two bounded away, Victor jumped in his van and started the engine.

"This never works." panted Jordan as the two continued to run down Pine street, approaching downtown. "I can't take another beating from these thugs."

"Save your breath, run." was all Ann said. As she began to speed up, the two ran across traffic while car horns blared. One car smashed into a stopped car in front of it. Jordan followed Ann step for step, not looking back to see how close Victor might be behind them. He failed to avoid the question lingering in his mind: What weapons might Victor have, and how far away was C.L. at this moment?

Traffic was on their side as they continued toward the waterfront. The two ran past stopped cars lined up and idling for blocks. They ignored walk signals, jumping in front of cars as they attempted to pull in to parking garages. So many cars, thought Jordan. Each with just one person inside, on their way to work. One person who was content with their life as a corporate drone. A cog in the wheel of Capitalism. How did they not revolt? How could they possibly be content with such a meaningless life? Who will care after they die? Not their employer, their employer will have just hired a replacement. Yet they insisted on worshipping their corporation like a god. There seemed to be an infinite supply of people willing to sacrifice their lives for a little bit of transient material wealth. Jordan couldn't understand, couldn't comprehend their reasoning. His brain didn't work that way. He couldn't help but see the larger picture, how his one short, precious life was the only opportunity he had to do something good for this world.

But where had all this noble ambition got him? In debt, unemployed and running from a pornographer. Maybe he didn't have things as figured out as he thought he did. Maybe he should have just faked contentment and prayed that it magically became real. No, he couldn't abandon his purpose that easily. Jordan couldn't live with himself, not for more than a month, trying to live that life. He had tried. Again and again he tried to be "normal" but it never worked. He couldn't ignore his soul for very long. His higher purpose was not giving up on him, no matter how many times he gave up on it.

But this life, what was he doing to make the world a better place with it? Making a porno was certainly not going to serve his goals any more than becoming a corporate cog would. But he didn't want to die an early death for unpaid drug debt either. There had to be a way to contribute something. Working at the coffee shop wasn't much, but at least he was doing something, trying to spread a little love in people's lives. He vividly remembered his first day working for Ali, the man practically saved his life. He was so fortunate to find someone who shared his higher purpose and wanted to help build a more loving community. What happened? Where had he gone wrong?

"Quick!" Ann shouted, as she leaped in front of an approaching train. Jordan followed and made it across with only moments to spare. They were at the waterfront now. Ann continued running and led Jordan behind a building along the boardwalk. It was quiet here, the ocean water gently splashed against the wooden posts of the dock. No one else was back here. The long freight train they had passed continued to noisily roll by, blocking all inbound traffic.

Ann leaned against the building, catching her breath, and said "We have to get out of Seattle."

"And go where? I have five dollars to my name. I don't know anyone outside of this city."

"Money is not that important, Jordan." she responded, standing up straight and scoping out the area. Ann turned toward the water and began running toward a pier. Jordan resumed following her and on the other side of the building a pair of tour boats rocked gently as they sat tied up to the dock. Ann leaped over the gate and ran down the gangway onto one of the boats with remarkable dexterity, as silently as a ninja.

Jordan was not capable of ninja-like stealth, but did his best to board the boat without being detected. Once onboard, he looked up at the pier they had descended from and saw that no one seemed to have noticed them. Ann opened the door to a storage room full of life vests and signaled for Jordan to follow her in.

"Is this boat even going anywhere? It's empty." he asked.

"I don't know, but I don't think Victor will find us here for the moment. How much do you owe C.L.?"

"About ten grand. You?"

"I was a distributor. I "lost" three hundred grand for a shipment last week."

"Holy shit! And he goes after you the same way he goes after me? I shouldn't have followed you. Fuck."

"Calm down, Jordan. I did more research than you did before I screwed him over. I know how he operates. This is a life insurance scheme. We might as well already be dead."

"Huh?"

"He owns the studio. He hires us as employees and takes out life insurance policies on us, as well as all of the regular employees. Once the policy is in effect, he arranges for our 'accidental' death. Then he collects the insurance money. This porn gig isn't about earning back what we owe him, we are just tokens in an insurance scheme to repay our debts with our lives."

"Fuck, wasn't that on NCIS once?"

"I don't know, it's not that original of an idea. I'm sure he's not the only one doing it. Who cares? We need to get the fuck out of here."

"Yeah, but how? Where?"

CHAPTER SIX

THE LIFE JACKET STORAGE CLOSET that Ann and Jordan now found themselves in had a single lightbulb mounted to the center of the ceiling. Ann had illuminated the bulb by flipping a switch inside the doorway. Surrounded by life jackets on all three remaining sides of the room, each of their faces appeared with an orange glow as they stood facing each other in the tiny space. With their backs against opposing walls of vests, there was only six inches of space between them.

Jordan now had time to examine Ann for the first time. Beads of sweat covered her face. Her short hair was held back behind her head in a ponytail, it appeared dark in color but had traces of dye and it was impossible to make out the actual color with the overwhelming orange hue of the room. Her pale, bony shoulders were exposed by light blue tank top she wore. Her arms bulged with toned muscles, as did her lower legs exposed below cut-off jean shorts. A pair of dirty Converse shoes completed her wardrobe. Ann's eyes stared piercingly into Jordan's, as if he were a crossword puzzle with one word remaining to fill in.

"Do you have any dust?" asked Jordan.

Ann sighed, shaking her head. "I'm not a junkie like you, Jordan. I'm a distributor. I do this for the money, it's the best job I could find. I don't use and I don't have any dust on me. Delivering my last supply is how I made the score that these guys are after me for. I was supposed to meet C.L. with the payment a week ago, I didn't realize how quickly he would turn on me."

Ann noticed Jordan's hands shaking and despite the orange illumination of the room, she could see his skin had a pale complexion. The sweat covering his body created a single placid layer, a polish on top of the ghost-white skin below. She watched him for a few more moments as his body gradually fell into a slump and he collapsed to the floor.

"You're going through withdrawal, aren't you? How long has it been?" she asked.

"Two days. I haven't gone this long without dust in years. C.L. always kept me supplied, even when I couldn't pay. If I don't get something soon this is going to be bad."

"We can't waste time trying to keep you high, Jordan. We are hiding under C.L.'s boot and enemies of whatever organization he is a part of. Let's find you some water, this boat doesn't seem to be going anywhere."

Ann cracked the door open and peeked her head out, no one was in sight. The boat slowly rocked back and forth with the waves as it sat docked and empty just as it was when they had boarded. There were three decks and they were on the bottom one, with the pier looming a dozen feet above them. She slowly, quietly opened the door and turned off the light in the storage closet. She stepped out and nodded at Jordan to follow her. He wearily stood up and complied.

Seventeen paces down the side of the ship they came to the restrooms with a drinking fountain standing between the mens and ladies rooms. Ann took the first drink, gulping down water for what felt like ten minutes to Jordan. When she lifted her head up and signaled for Jordan to take a drink he didn't hesitate to quench his thirst, hoping the water might also relieve the pain of the beating C.L. had given him and the inferno burning within his mind, demanding its missed dose of dust. He continued drinking water until the flow from the fountain lost pressure and faded to a drizzle.

Looking up at Ann, he questioned her "Now what? When does this ship leave? Where will it take us?"

"Fuck if I know. It doesn't appear to be going anywhere anytime soon. Maybe we need to find an alternative plan."

"We could try to hop on a bus to Portland."

"That's just jumping from the frying pan into the fire. You know that's where one of C.L.'s main hubs is, don't you?"

"All I know is that C.L.'s street team brings me my drugs on a regular basis. I don't know where they come from. What about heading up to Canada?"

"And then what, Jordan? You think they'll grant us asylum running from a drug dealer? You think C.L. doesn't know anyone in Canada? You don't think things through much, do you?"

"Do you have a better idea or do you want to just keep knocking mine down?"

"You're not going to like my idea." Ann responded,

pausing before she continued, "I say we stay and fight. I'm not going to live my life on the run, looking behind my back."

"You mean go to the cops?"

"Hell no, they'll just lock us up. I'm saying we tell C.L., Victor and whoever else these thugs wants to send our way to go fuck themselves."

"That hasn't worked out very well for me so far." Jordan responded, pointing to the sweltering burn on his nose.

"Do you have a phone?" Ann asked as she stretched out her hand, passively demanding he hand it to her. Jordan pulled a black smartphone from his pocket and surrendered it to her with a confused, questioning gaze. She turned it on and began dialing a phone number, then put the phone to her ear and walked into the ladies room. Jordan didn't move.

Five minutes later, Ann exited the ladies room and the phone was nowhere to be seen. She walked past Jordan and signaled for him to follow her.

"Hey, I never agreed to go along with this crazy plan of yours! It's not even a plan, it's just a stupid idea. You're going to get us killed."

"Do you have a better idea? If not, shut up and follow me."

Jordan followed Ann up to the second deck. They were now level with the pier, but there was no gangway to exit the ship on this deck, the one they had used to board the ship went down to the deck below. As Ann scanned the pier she turned to Jordan and simply said "Wait."

Jordan slid down to sit on the floor. The shaking had

gone from his hands to his entire arms. He was drenched in sweat and went between burning up and freezing from moment to moment. He felt dizzy and as he looked out on the dock his vision became blurry until he blinked a few times, then it restored to clarity, but only briefly. He thought about his predicament, there had to be a way to escape. Fighting back was pointless, it was basically suicide. There had to be somewhere he could go. Ohio. What harm could possibly come to him in Ohio? He could steal a car and drive to Ohio. Start a new life. Find a new dealer and be diligent not to get into debt with him. Work at a coffee shop. Live a simple, relaxed life. Maybe even meet a woman.

What about doing some good in the world? That noble cause he loved to stand on a pedestal and defend, but never did anything about. Could he ever do any good in this world? Was killing C.L., or at least fending him off, a feat that would make the world a better place? How could he do some good for once, whether here or otherwise? The more he thought about it, the more he came to believe that nothing he as an individual could do would have much of an impact on the world. He needed to find some like-minded people to really start a revolution. After all, a revolution was what he wanted, wasn't it? No revolution ever succeeded with just one person leading the charge. Would Ann help him? She seemed to be solely concerned with making money. If she was so happy with her drug income, why did she steal from C.L.? She knew that would end things. What was her idea here? Her story didn't make any sense.

"Why did you rip off C.L.?" Jordan asked.

"We don't have time to discuss that, Jordan. Just wait, someone is coming to get us any minute now. Be quiet."

"No, answer my question, Ann. Why did you rip off C.L.? If things were going so well, why did you throw a wrench in them?"

"It's not just me, Jordan. I'm in a group working to overthrow the whole network. We all withheld payment from him at the same time, shorting him over ten million. That's all I can tell you right now."

"Ten million?! What is my ten grand in the picture of that shortage? I'm not joining you guys, your the ones he wants to kill, not me. Fuck, I bet he would pay me to turn you in. Give me my phone back, I'm done with this bullshit."

"I flushed your phone. You are free to leave, but if you do then you will just have C.L. and all of us after you. Is that your latest winning strategy?"

"Fine." Jordan responded in defeat, he remained slumped on the floor, closing his eyes and breathing deeply. He felt completely defeated.

"Now!" Ann shouted as she pulled him to his feet. A black sedan was stopped along the boardwalk and before Jordan knew what to do he saw Ann jump from the side of the ship on to the pier. He scrambled to follow her, falling disgracefully chest-first onto the dock, pushing himself up he saw Ann open the rear door of the sedan and gesture for him to get in. He dashed to the car and got in, closing the door behind him.

CHAPTER SEVEN

ALI HAD BEEN TROUBLED ALL day, he was slightly distracted and lacked his usual enthusiasm when greeting customers. His distraction was not an impediment to Hannah's training as she was able to pick up most things on her own. Sensing Ali's disinterest in talking, Hannah occupied herself through the work day trying to figure out what was bothering him, she believed it must have something to do with Jordan.

"Why did you fire that guy?" she questioned him.

"He's no good, Hannah. He shows up late, high, covered in shit. Customer service is a foreign language to him. I can't afford to have someone like that in my store."

"But why today? And wish such gusto? You could have told him privately, given him time to find another job."

"You don't need to defend this guy, Hannah. It's over. We move on. Let me show you the afternoon cleaning routine."

"It's been on your mind all day, it's been troubling you Ali. Anyone who looks at you can tell. There has to be more to the story than you're letting on."

Ali walked into the back room without responding. The store was empty, an early afternoon lull setting in between lunch and coffee break time for the nine to fivers, their primary clientele. The only sounds were the classic rock radio coming from the speakers overhead and the drone of the fans attempting to keep the shop cool in the midst of a brutal summer heatwave. Hannah followed Ali into the back room. Just as he was showing her where the cleaning supplies were kept the front door of the store slammed open and the shouting of an angry man erupted "Ali! You here?"

Ali looked down at the floor with regret, the intrusion didn't seem to catch him by surprise as it did Hannah. This had not been the first day she had in mind, she reflected. Calmly, but on guard, Ali looked at Hannah and whispered for her to stay put. He walked back out to the front of the store and addressed the intruder, "What can I do for you sir?"

"Has Jordan come by? Did you tell him about me?" the voice shouted back.

"No, no – I let him go this morning. He's your problem now, not mine."

"Are you lying to me? Nice guy trying to protect his deadbeat employee? Don't fuck with me, grandpa."

"Calm down, put the gun away. I did just as you told me, what more do you want?" came Ali's trembling voice.

"Show me your back room, now." The man demanded.

Overhearing the conversation while still standing in the back room, Hannah went into full on panic. Adrenaline rushed through her blood stream, she could hear the stream of blood flowing past her eardrums. She had never had anything like this happen in her five years working at the college cafe. Who was this Ali guy? How could such a seemingly great man get caught up with a junkie like

Jordan and whoever this gun slinging madman was? She didn't ever consider that her job as a barista would be a high risk one. Leaning against a refrigerator she evaluated her options. Finally she considered what Ali would want her to do and without hesitation she withdrew her phone from her front pocket and dialed the police.

When the operator answered she swallowed the knot in her throat and whispered "Help, gun." then hung up her phone and returned it to her pocket as she heard Ali opening the door to the back room.

"Just my new employee back here, sir. Look, enough with the rampage. You've scared the crap out of us, intimidated us. What do you want from me?" Ali pleaded with the man as they entered the back room.

Hannah's hands were shaking, she looked at the man, veins seeming to pop from his face, pricks of hair emerging from his nearly bald head. Gun in his right hand, he appeared like an angry baboon searching for a fight. Her gaze slowly drifted down to the ground as she closed her eyes and prayed silently for this all to come to an end.

The angry man walked around the tiny storage room, searching for Jordan. Apparently suspecting that he shrunk down to the size of a basketball and was just hiding on one of the shelves. He was buying time, this must have been his last hope in his search for Jordan and he had been defeated.

"Call me if you hear from him." the man said, then proceeded to stomp out of the back room.

"Drop the gun, hands up, get on your knees!" came a shout from the front of the store. The police had arrived. Hannah breathed a sigh of relief. Ali looked more panic stricken than he had when the angry man was threatening him. The man dropped to his knees and the clink of his gun bouncing off the concrete floor indicated he had surrendered.

Ali and Hannah stayed in the back room. Ali looked questioningly at Hannah.

"I thought it would be what you wanted me to do." She responded before he asked the question.

Ali smiled back at her, nodding. Then signaled for her to stay put. He slowly crept out of the back room.

"On your knees!" shouted an overzealous police officer as Ali emerged. He dropped to his knees slowly, reaching an arm down for support to relieve his elderly ankles and knees.

Looking up at the officer, he calmly stated "I'm the shop owner."

"Is there anyone else in the store?" responded a voice Hannah had not heard yet, there must have been at least three police officers.

"My employee, in the back room."

Not knowing what to do, Hannah froze and slunk down to the floor trembling.

Foot steps approached and a young police officer, not yet 30 years old, entered with his gun drawn but pointed at the floor. He signaled for her to follow him out to the store front. She slowly rose up and followed him, her limbs felt as if they made of material lighter than air. Every ounce of her body was trembling as she looked around the store and saw the angry baboon on his knees, hands cuffed behind his head. The young officer signaled for her to sit at a table and then told Ali to join her.

Within minutes, the louder officer was escorting the intruder out to his squad car and driving away. Meanwhile another two officers had pulled up in a white unmarked Dodge Charger. The younger officer sat down at the table with Ali and Hannah and the two new officers stood by the store entrance, turning away curious onlookers and potential customers.

"Do you know that man?" asked the younger officer.

"He's my roaster. Upset I was behind with payments. He over-reacted. Threatening me." Ali lied.

"Your roaster? Are you sure? What's his name?"

"Jake. Jake Cumberbatch."

"Are you sure? His ID says his name is Craig Ladro Ferrari, not Jake Cumberbatch."

Ali sighed, his ruse so quickly spoiled. He responded solemnly to the officer, "I'm sorry. I should have been honest with you. I don't know the man well, but I don't want any undue trouble for him. He called me last night, I don't know his name. He told me to fire my employee or he would break into my store and ransack it. I did what he said, but he came back today claiming I deceived him."

Purple Haze came on to the radio in the background. The fans continued to whirr, a weak attempt at keeping the temperature in the store down. Hannah was relieved to finally hear the full story about Jordan's dismissal from Ali, disappointed that it took the police to get it out of him. Clearly he didn't fully trust her yet. She gazed out the open window and watched a man on a skateboard roll down the hill in the bike lane.

"Call us if you hear from Craig or any of his associates." the young police officer responded, handing Ali a business card.

"Wait!" responded Ali. "Do you know more about this guy? Who is he? What business does he have with my employee?"

"He's no good. But he won't bother you anymore. Hire your employee back." the officer said as he walked toward the door, exiting the shop with the other two officers that had been standing guard.

Ali looked at Hannah, raising his eyes in bewilderment. "I think we can call it a day." he told her.

Hannah helped Ali close up the shop early, both of them operated in near silence as Hendrix continued to play on the radio. Hannah had survived a first day that she would never forget.

"It's okay if you don't want to come back, I know this isn't what you signed up for. You won't believe me, but I swear to you it's never been like this. You had a strange first day." Ali told her in the most apologetic tone he could muster.

"I'll see you in the morning, Ali." Hannah responded, looking up into his weary eyes. She gave him a hug, then turned and began walking toward her flat.

Ali took his phone from his pocket and called Jordan as he stood in the empty store. The phone rang to voicemail, he left a brief message telling Jordan to call him back. Sighing, he placed the phone back in his pocket, left the shop and locked the door behind him.

CHAPTER EIGHT

A S THE SEDAN JETTED INTO traffic driving down the waterfront, Jordan fastened his seatbelt. Looking at the two men driving and Ann in the seat next to him, he felt entirely out of place. The men were too clean cut, Ann was too calm, this didn't feel like a getaway in the middle of a drug war, this felt like a corporate exec on her way to work, with a junkie along for the ride. The two men up front were completely silent. Jordan could see an earpiece in the right ear of the driver. He looked at Ann, who was staring out the window, she looked serene and at peace.

"We're going somewhere safe, Jordan. I'll help you get through your withdrawal, then you're on your own." she said, without moving her gaze from the window.

Unsure how to respond and utterly exhausted, Jordan settled into his leather seat and closed his eyes as the car left the city, crossing the lake that separated Seattle from its suburbs.

He awoke as the car pulled to a stop in front of a large mansion. The entryway door was open and a young man stood on the steps. Ann rushed out of the car and up the steps, embracing the man as if she hadn't seen him in ages. Jordan was slower to climb out of the car, having just awoken from the best slumber he had experienced in days. After he exited and closed the door behind him the car drove off.

The house was exquisite, Jordan had never seen anything like it. Built from large stone blocks, with a circular tower in one corner, complete with arrow slits and a large blue flag flying from the top, it was half-castle half-mansion. The windows were divided into small panes with gothic triangular stone arches above them. Inside, a giant chandelier illuminated the dining room. The windows into the two floors above were dark.

Ann waved Jordan to come inside from the stairs leading up to the entrance. Jordan turned and began walking toward her and the man who must be her husband he surmised. As he approached he saw the intricate carving in the entryway doors depicting angels fighting demons atop a giant mountain, it was a masterpiece. He looked up to Ann, glanced at the man, and then returned his gaze to Ann questioningly.

"This is Ricky, my husband. Ricky, this is Jordan. I ran into him at work today and he needs a place to rest for the night."

Ricky looked at Jordan, slowly inspecting him from head to toe, like a stray dog. He nodded, and reached his hand out in greeting.

As the three entered the house, Jordan was awestruck as he stared at the marble fireplace, it contained real wood and real fire that crackled as it lit up the living room. The fireplace was bigger than any he had seen before, it stood taller than he was and wide enough to fit a car inside. As his gaze wandered up to the ceiling, he admired the stained oak boards and large cedar support beams. He could smell the combination of the burning wood from the fireplace and cooking meat coming from the kitchen. Large, plush leather armchairs were scattered around the living room and seemed to be begging him to sit and enjoy them. As he walked toward the one with a large ottoman in front of it, he was interrupted by Ricky.

"Shoes, friend. Please take off your shoes."

Jordan didn't have to be asked twice, kicking off his sneakers and resuming his journey to the chair. As he approached it, he ran his hand over the cracked leather and admired how soft it felt to the touch. Not hesitating another moment, he sank into the chair and put his feet up on the ottoman. Letting out a deep breath that seemed to have been held within him all day, every worry and care seemed to suddenly float away.

"Are you hungry Jordan? Care to join us for dinner? Our chef is roasting some chicken and vegetables."

Jordan pondered whether this was what the big time in the drug world was like. Ricky seemed too short and well-mannered to be a drug king, he was just as out of place in the underworld as Ann was. The meal sounded delicious, it was the first time he could recall craving real food in months. His body seemed to yearn for the nutrients, a voice in his soul finally awakening from the clouds of dust that had previously drowned it out. Jordan looked over to Ricky and nodded a simple "Yes."

Ann and Ricky joined Jordan in the living room. Sitting together on a love seat facing Jordan, they looked at him like an adopted puppy, with more pity than love. A man walked in and addressed Ricky directly. "Perhaps your visitor would like a bath? I've taken the liberty to run one in the ground floor guest quarters, sir."

Ricky looked to Jordan, raising his eyebrow into a question mark. As Jordan imagined the cleansing purity of a bath a rush of electricity bounded through his soul, providing a spark of inner warmth he had not felt in ages. Without a word, he got up from the chair and stood in front of the butler. "Show me the way!" he responded.

After Jordan emerged from his bath and put on a clean set of clothes that had been laid out for him, he followed the sound of Ann and Ricky's voices into the kitchen where the two were seated at a small dining table filled with steaming platters of food. He sat down to join them and Ricky started the conversation by asking Jordan how he met Ann, but Ann interrupted before Jordan had a chance to formulate a response.

"My exit didn't go as smoothly as we had hoped, I picked up Jordan along the way."

Ricky continued questioning Jordan, "You're not with the agency then, are you?" Mocking surprise.

"Agency? Is that what you call your drug ring? No, I'm a customer, I don't get mixed up with the business."

"Oh, don't be foolish, Jordan! You got mixed up with the business when you fell into debt with C.L. and you know it." piped up Ann.

Jordan sought to change the topic as quickly as possible, asking Ann "Why are we even at your house? Surely C.L. will find us here."

"C.L. is locked up for the night, and this house is well protected." Ann responded.

"Let's lighten up the conversation and enjoy this meal,

you've both been through the ringer and look exhausted. How about this heat?" interrupted Ricky.

"I'm not interested in talking about the weather poindexter. You two don't run a drug ring, there ain't no way. Tell me what's going on here!"

"Calm down, Jordan." responded Ann. "You're right, we don't run a drug ring. Ricky is the CEO of Facefeed, that's where this house came from, legitimate money. I work for the DEA. I've been working undercover to breakdown C.L.'s organization."

"You're a cop?! Fuck! What the fuck." Jordan stood up from his chair and began pacing across the kitchen.

"Jordan, chill out. You're over-emotional and tense from the withdrawal."

"Chill out? I've gone from under the thumb of my dealer to under the nose of law. I'm fucked! Shit, I need to get out of here!"

"The DEA doesn't give a fuck about some low-level dust fiend, Jordan. You're safer here than you are out there. Sit down. I'll explain." Ann commanded.

Jordan seemed to be having an argument in his head, shaking it violently back and forth as he paced across the kitchen. Finally reasoning that Ann was right, he sat back down and resumed eating, awaiting Ann's explanation.

"Victor picked me up and I mistakenly thought he was my escort from deep cover. Instead I met you and Miss Q. I could have just left you at the coffee shop, but I saw a glimmer of hope in your soul. There's more to you than you let on, Jordan. You don't have to live the life of a junkie, working coffee shops and running away from dust dealers. I know you could be more, and that spark in your eye told me you wanted to be more."

"You want me to flip? Join the fuzz? Forget it."

"No, you're jumping to conclusions without listening. Listen to me Jordan."

Ann's language reminded Jordan of Fiona, always seeing more in him than he saw in himself. He had not been spoken to like this since she left him. As his thoughts drifted to his lost love her image appeared in his mind and stared him in the eyes as it did earlier that day, looking at him with stone cold solemnity, she slowly said "Listen." and finally the urgency and fear that had rapt his mind since learning that Ann was a cop vanished and for the first time he just sat and listened.

"Ricky and I met in college. He was studying Computer Science and I was studying Criminal Justice. We were both taking a required English course, European Literature with Professor White. Our fields did not define us. We both wanted to make a real difference in the world. We were inspired by the epic stories of revolution and peaceful coexistence, especially Siddhartha. We wanted to devote our lives to making the world better for everyone. That's why I joined the D.E.A. and Ricky started Facefeed. That revolutionary spark has led us both to great success, launching a fortune 500 company and bringing down one of the largest drug rings on the west coast. I saw that same desire for good in you, Jordan. It's a soul-spark that some people have and some people don't. Those who have it see it in others the instant they look into their eyes. I see it as my duty when I encounter others with the spark to help them realize their dreams. We have started a foundation to help inspired children get into college and realize their dreams the same way we have. It's our life passion. We're here to help you Jordan."

Jordan laughed so hard a half-chown grain of rice shot from his nose.

"Help me, eh? You think you're just a bunch of do-gooders out saving the world? You think the war on drugs and invention of social media are making the world a better place? You're just as fucking stupid as everyone else out there." Jordan jolted upright as his mind ignited with rage.

"You see my soul-spark? Well, I don't see yours. Masking your material success and selfishness with bullshit world-saving rhetoric may make it past the magazine writers desperate to sell ads with an inspiring article, but you won't make it past me.

"You, Ricky, you just suck kids' brains out and turn them into mush the same way television did for our generation. And you, Ann, you think locking up drug dealers helps anyone? How about helping the addicts? Providing some recovery support and housing? Neither of you are changing a damn thing. You really want to do some good? Then you must stop worshipping the capitalist system and see how it's destroying the world, not saving it. If you ever get that far, then perhaps you can help me wake up more souls. It's only a revolution that will save this world. Not an app or a strategic arrest. You're fools."

Jordan got up, disgusted, and walked back to the guest suite where he had bathed before dinner. He shut the door to the room behind him and fell down to his knees on the ground. Frustrated beyond control with how even those with good intentions were doing more harm than good and didn't even know it, he felt utterly hopeless. Laying on his hands and knees, breathing deeply, he began pounding on the carpeted floor and screaming with the rage that was burning in his soul. He continued to wail and beat the floor until he felt completely defeated and collapsed, drifting into a deep sleep.

CHAPTER NINE

TRAVELING THROUGH SPACE SO RAPIDLY that stars blurred into strips of white light, Jordan attempted to take in his surroundings, but there were none. As he continued traveling through space, he attempted to adjust the direction he was heading, he tried to swing his arms, shift his entire body, focus his mind in a particular direction, but no matter what he did or thought he continued traveling in the same direction. Looking ahead, he didn't see anything in particular, just a never-ending void.

With a loud, but undramatic 'pop' sound he was suddenly standing still and surrounded by a dark green marsh. Ancient trees surrounded him in all directions, they were covered in moss with long branches hanging draped across multiple younger, smaller branches. The marsh waters sat still, the surface was covered in lily pads and other sea growth. The air was warm and humid, it appeared to be mid-day but there was no direct sunlight owing to the dense tree cover. Jordan was naked.

A leprechaun emerged from behind a tree. "Where are your trousers?" he asked, taking stock of the human visitor.

Jordan began dancing uncontrollably, his legs bounding from beneath him and his arms moving in rapid, robotic motions. As he continued to dance in front of the leprechaun his voice echoed, "From the trees grow paper in purple yellow sticky lenses for Atlantis."

The mushrooms growing from the base of nearly every tree began glowing bright neon green, purple, and blue. As Jordan's dancing continued the mushrooms seemed to grow larger and brighter. Jordan began spinning around the trees and continued to babble incomprehensible phrases as the leprechaun looked on in awe.

Monkeys emerged from their hiding places in the trees and looked on at Jordan and the magic mushrooms. Suddenly, one leaped down in front of him and began to join him in dancing. Then another monkey leaped down, and in rapid succession dozens of monkeys joined Jordan in his dance. More mushrooms began popping up from the forest floor and rapidly growing, aglow with bright effervescent colors, some were spotted and others were polk-a-dotted.

The leprechaun stood motionless and repeated his query, "Where are your trousers?"

Suddenly a group of men and women, as naked as the day they were born, walked up to investigate the commotion. Carrying hand drums and other wooden instruments, they took in all the dancing and wild fungi, then began to play music in rhythm with Jordan's dancing.

As the dancing and music continued, Jordan's singing turned into primitive guttural throat chanting and strange noise making. He began jumping up and propelling himself from tree to tree. As each foot bounced from tree trunk to tree trunk, bright green footprints were left in the moss, glowing for seconds and fading as he continued to fly through the forest.

Aglow with the spirit, the naked musicians began to dance while continuing to play their instruments in a fast-paced syncopated rhythm. The monkeys bounced between tree branches and the ground, spinning in mid-air and waving their arms wildly as they flew. The leprechaun remained motionless and silent, taking in all of the singing and dancing that surrounded him. Scratching the whiskers on his chin, he looked up at Jordan and asked a third time, "Where are your trousers?"

As the mushrooms continued to grow they became as tall as Jordan and the luminance from their glow began to outshine the setting sun and reflected off the moss of the surrounding trees, turning the forest into a multi-colored neon discotec. Looking up through the tree branches, Jordan could see the stars in the night sky and noticed that they still appeared as white streaks, suggesting the speed at which he was still traveling through outer space, albeit on this newfound marshland with all of these other creatures.

One of the trees closest to the leprechaun began moving slowly, at first suggesting a strong breeze coming through the marsh, but as it continued to sway back and forth its roots came up through the forest floor and sprouted into legs. The tree continued swaying and began to spin and join in the dancing along with Jordan, the monkeys and the naked musicians. Soon other trees were uprooting themselves and joining in the party too. As they began dancing, their branches lit up in neon browns and greens, further illuminating the forest. A mighty, thumping bass-tone was emitted as each root-bundle foot struck the ground while the trees continued dancing in rhythm with the musicians.

Jordan climbed up one of the dancing trees and continued to dance while atop a large branch, clapping his hands in the air and shouting in song with the rhythm of the forest. Owls circled overhead observing the event and growing in number as more flew in. While the stars continued moving past in rapid blurs, a full moon could be seen overhead, large and bright with a yellowish glow, it was enormous, a harvest moon. Jordan jumped up to higher and higher branches, but he could not stop staring at the moon. His shouting and singing turned into howls as he rose to the top of the forest and could see over all the surrounding trees. His howls were soon accompanied by distant wolves.

Continuing to look up at the moon, Jordan noticed a giant crevasse emerge on its surface, forming into a smile. Two craters materialized in place of eyes and the smile grew broader as the moon looked down upon Jordan. He continued howling at it, in chorus with a growing number of wolves near and far. Dozens of trees were now dancing and their motion and glow as seen from above formed a giant spinning chaos.

Feeling the enormous power of the spirit that tingled through his entire body, from the tip of his head to each of his toes, Jordan felt so powerful and at peace with the world he lifted his feet from the tree he stood atop and drifted into mid-air, continuing to dance and sing.

Suddenly, a witch on a broomstick flew by and wrapped her arm around his neck. Jordan looked up at his captor and she shouted back down at him "Jordan, wake up! Where are your trousers?"

CHAPTER TEN

JORDAN AWOKE AS ANN WAS pulling him up from the floor and resting his back against the base of the bed he had not slept in. His trousers indeed appeared to be missing.

"Did you sleep on the floor all night?"

"I must have fallen asleep there. Rather comfortable carpeting."

"And your pants?"

"No idea, Ann! But I had the most wonderful dream, it was magical! I must draw it out before I forget it. Quick, fetch me a pen and paper!"

"Pants don't just disappear. Do you want some bacon and eggs? Ricky is in the kitchen preparing breakfast."

"Pen. Paper. Now. Please!"

Impatient, Jordan stood up and walked past Ann out of the bedroom. Entering the kitchen in his boxer shorts and t-shirt, he asked Ricky "Have you got a pen and a pad?"

Ricky looked up from the frying pan, startled to see Jordan with no pants on. "In my office, bud. Up the stairs on the right."

Jordan leaped from the kitchen up the stairs. Sitting

at Ricky's desk with pen in hand, he began drawing out the scenes from his dream. He had never drawn anything before, but this was not an experience he wanted to forget and drawing seemed to be the best way to preserve the memory. Upon finishing a handful of sketches, he looked down and was impressed with how well they turned out for his lack of drawing experience. He felt fulfilled in a way he had never felt before. No high, no ecstasy, no bliss could contend with the energy he felt in his heart. Artistically fulfilled.

He walked back down the steps, sketches in hand, and Ann greeted him holding a pair of trousers in her hands.

The bacon and eggs were delicoius, Jordan couldn't recall the last time he had eaten a wholesome hot breakfast. Most of his time was spent getting high, eating was a subordinate activity no more interesting or appealing than voiding his bowels.

"How are you feeling, Jordan?" asked Ricky.

"That was quite an episode last night, but you are hardly to blame, dust withdrawal is brutal on the nerves." Ann chimed in before Jordan could respond.

"I feel amazing! I'm sorry for being such an ass last night after you offered me so much hospitality."

"You weren't entirely in the wrong, Jordan. You brought up some fair points, albeit with undue attitude. I have often wondered if I'm really making the world a better place with Facefeed. I truly believe greater connectedness enhances the human experience, and we are doing lots of work to bring the Internet to under-served regions. But I'm curious, for all your complaining you don't seem to offer many solutions. Tell me your great ideas to make the world a better place, Jordan. Perhaps we could work together."

Jordan paused. The truth was he never really could come up with any great solutions. In the past, he had always laughed this sort of question off, claiming that if it was so easy to find a solution to the world's problems, someone would have done it by now. But if there was really nothing that could be done, he might as well off himself. Deep down he believed there was a solution and he had hope that he could make a difference. Beyond that, he had no real answers. However, motivated by his inspiring dream and artistic creation, he was determined to come up with a compelling answer for Ricky. He went back through his rant from last night and recalled his deep desire to wake Ann and Ricky from their false belief that they were already saving the world.

"We must wake people up to reality." he responded.

"How? Aren't there already hundreds of non-profits and documentary films failing to do that?"

"Yes, you're right. True awakening requires more direct, forceful, perhaps even violent action."

"Like what?" asked Ann hesitantly.

"Shutting down the distractions. Forcing people to emerge from their digital cocoons of illusion and entertainment. We must give them no option but to see reality."

"Then you think they'll do something? Or just become miserably depressed like you?"

"I'm not depressed, Ann. If I didn't have hope I wouldn't be here, I would have given up."

"Haven't you given up already? What good have you done? Isn't your dust just another distraction?"

Jordan bowed his head down, nodding. He knew she was right, he was just as distracted as everyone else. Truth is, he was worse than they were. While he was aware of the vast problems facing humanity and believed he could do something to improve the situation, he chose to distract himself instead. He was waiting for others to join him because he felt utterly helpless on his own and that's what drove him to the dust.

"You're right, I can't deny it. But if there was something I could do, I would do it. There is a solution, I just can't do it on my own. No revolution started single-handedly. I need help."

"That's for sure." Ricky replied with a laugh. Ann and Jordan looked back at him shamefully.

"How do you suppose we stop the distractions?" asked Ann.

"Cut the Internet, turn off the TV, disable the gas pumps and destroy the electric grid." Jordan said bluntly.

"That will certainly require more than just you, Jordan. That is next to impossible, even with my money and an army of revolutionaries." remarked Ricky.

"It's the only way." sighed Jordan.

"Maybe. What if we had an "Unplug Day" and encouraged people to disconnect for the day. I could fund the marketing and give you free ads on Facefeed."

"No, you don't get it. Forget it." Jordan responded with frustration, "If people would voluntarily cut themselves off, this wouldn't be a problem. It would mean that they already saw through the distractions, it would mean they're already in touch with reality. That's the problem, they are utterly ignorant. It has to be forced."

"You're talking about terrorism." said Ann.

"No, it's only terrorism if you mean to cause harm. I mean to awaken people to reality. No harm. This is not terrorism."

"The FBI won't see it that way."

"I'll fight it to the bitter end in court, and if they really want to lock me up, despite my not harming a single human soul, so be it."

Ann and Ricky were speechless.

"It's civil disobedience, that's all. Yes, I want to break some laws, but it's for the greater good."

"Have you ever tried to do this before?"

"I looked in to shutting off the Internet. It's not as hard as you might think. Most people use Conblast for their Internet service at home. If we shut down a few of their central data centers, we would basically be shutting down Internet for the entire country."

Ricky nodded. "You're right, but you underestimate how easy it is to gain access to and disable their data centers. It would probably be easier to hack them virtually than physically."

"Perhaps, in either case it would require skills beyond my ability."

"Yeah, mine too." Ricky responded. "Listen, I've got to get to the office. Ann, can you drop off Jordan or should I ask Jeeves?"

"Drop him where, Ricky? This kid needs help, he still has a drug gang after him. I'm not just throwing him to the wolves."

"Fine, well I've got to go. Don't leave him in the house alone."

Ann waved goodbye to her husband, half mockingly.

Clearly irritated by his patronizing attitude. She looked at Jordan after Ricky had departed. "I have an all-day debrief to attend, I've been under cover for months. Do you want to come to the DEA office? Strangely, it is probably the safest place for you right now."

Unable to think of any better options, Jordan nodded. He collected his sketches and followed Ann out of the house.

CHAPTER ELEVEN

A S THEY WERE SPEEDING DOWN the highway in the same black sedan that had picked them up from the waterfront, driven by what appeared to be the same nondescript man with an earpiece and his co-pilot, Jordan noticed a familiar dark red van pull up along side them. The passenger window of the van rolled down, revealing C.L.'s unmistakeable mug, his lips parted as he licked them, like a dog who had just discovered two unattended strips of bacon.

Without warning, the van slammed into the side of the sedan, making it slide into the guard rail. As the driver tried to correct course back on to the highway the van slammed into them again, this time with enough force that the car became lodged into the guard rail and its engine came to a stop. Jordan's head slammed back into the head-rest from whiplash, knocking his mind into a daze. As he recovered, he noticed that Ann was no longer sitting next to him and the man in the front passenger seat was also gone. As the sound of gunfire rang out, Jordan laid down in the back seat, attempting to avoid the melee.

Shots continued to fire back and forth, Jordan peeked

out of the door Ann had left ajar after her exit. He could see Ann wrestling with C.L. while C.L. continued to fire loosely aimed rounds at the man who had been sitting in the passenger seat. Jordan remained hidden, frozen and unsure how to proceed. Then he recalled Ann's words back on the boat about fighting back, about no longer living on the run. Having no weapons and no combat training, Jordan wasn't sure how he could be of any use here, but he refused to stay put. He looked up at the driver of the sedan and asked "Got anything I can use?"

"There's a tire iron in the trunk, pull down the seat to get at it. Might be some flares too."

Jordan crawled down to the footwell of the back seat and pulled down the backrest to gain access to the trunk. Inside he saw the tire iron and a pack of road flares. He grabbed the flares and snuck out his side of the car with just enough space between the guard rail and the door for him to exit.

He was now able to see the entire scene and spotted Victor sitting in the drivers seat of the van, exposed by the open passenger door. He sparked one of the flares, took aim and chucked it at Victor, then dodged back behind the car. Moments later, the loud "Fuck!" that erupted from the van indicated he had hit his target.

Looking out from under the rear bumper of the car, Jordan could see Ann and C.L. continuing to fight, it was unclear who was winning. Ann landed a roundhouse kick flat on C.L. face, knocking him to the ground. He grabbed Ann by the ankles dragging her down to the ground with him, only to be kicked in the groin as he was half way back up to standing.

Victor was still sitting in the drivers seat of the van and the flare only seemed to have aggravated him, having tossed it out of the van into oncoming traffic. Suddenly the sedan started and the driver shouted "Get in!" to Jordan.

Doing as instructed, he returned to the back seat of the car, head ducked down as shots resumed firing. After three more shots rang out, a painful cry erupted from C.L. At that moment the co-pilot returned to the passenger seat of the sedan, quickly followed by Ann who joined Jordan in the back. The doors closed and the sedan returned to the highway wearily, the body heavily damaged and smoke coming from the engine.

"Is he dead?" asked Jordan.

"Doubt it, but neither are we and I would like to keep it that way." responded Ann.

"How did they find us?"

"Probably tracked us from the dock yesterday and just waited for us to leave the compound."

"Who is he?" Jordan asked, pointing to the co-pilot sitting in front of him.

"My name is Jackson." the man responded.

"One of Ricky's security team, assigned to watch me. As if my DEA training wasn't enough to defend myself." Ann responded dismissively, then continued, "Apparently C.L. made bail. His organization is spiraling down the toilet, his boss can't be too happy."

"Why's he still after us?" questioned Jordan.

"He must think he can get the money back from me, save his neck."

"Where is the money?"

"DEA piggy bank, evidence."

"Did you keep any of it?"

"Why would I?" Ann asked.

Jordan sat silently without responding. The car continued down the highway until it arrived back in downtown Seattle, pulling into the gated and guarded parking garage of a high rise. Stopping in front of a guarded elevator, Ann exited and signaled for Jordan to join her. She flashed her badge to the guard and entered the elevator. As the doors of the elevator closed the sedan pulled away. Jordan wondered if they were used to seeing beat-up smoking cars pull in to the garage here.

The elevator stopped on the third floor of the building, revealing a lobby that looked no different than any other office lobby. Ann approached the receptionist's desk and introduced Jordan, asking if he could wait out here for the morning. The receptionist obliged and Ann told Jordan she would meet him here for lunch.

It was nine in the morning. Jordan had no intention of sitting in the lobby all morning with nothing to do. He asked the receptionist if he could use the phone, then dialed one of the few numbers he knew by heart.

"What?" answered the voice on the other end of the line.

"It's Jordan. I have information I think you might find valuable."

"The only thing you could possibly have of any value is the ten grand you owe me. And since you thought it was such a great idea to burn the skin off Victor's leg with a flare, your bill just doubled. If you don't work today, I will shoot you in the face myself. Now, where should I send Victor to pick you up?"

Jordan hung up the phone. He was in more of a bind than he thought he was. He sat down in the lobby to evaluate his options.

His ideas for escape were few and far between. After half an hour had passed with Jordan mostly staring at the ceiling, slowly moving his thumbs back and forth with fingers clasped together, the receptionist stood up to tell him he had a message from Ann.

"She says Ricky is sending a car for you, meet him on the 1st Ave entrance in five minutes."

Jordan decided to continue playing along, lacking any better options. He went out to the street and watched all the people walking past as he waited for the car. Most of them were staring at their cell phones, others were looking out in front of them, but had wires running into their ears. Reality was too much for most people to bear. Why? Jordan found it rather beautiful.

A dark blue BMW pulled up in front of him and the driver leaped out to greet Jordan.

"Jordan? Let me get that for you." the driver opened the rear passenger door.

"Can I sit in front? I've had enough of the back seat for one day."

"Suit yourself." the driver responded, opening the front passenger door for him.

As the driver got back into the car and pulled back onto the street he asked what type of music Jordan liked.

"G. Love and Special Sauce."

"You hear that Seary? Play some G. Love." the driver instructed the car.

"Calling Pam." the car responded.

"No, no, hang up. Fucking car."

"Where are we going?" asked Jordan.

"Facefeed offices in Fremont. We'll be there before you know it!"

They arrived at a nondescript building along the canal in Fremont. Feeling more and more like a twig afloat on the rapids without any hope of choosing his own path, Jordan entered the building and saw Ricky in the lobby waiting for him.

"What's up, Ricky?" Jordan asked as he entered the building.

"Hey, I was in my morning briefing and couldn't stop thinking about what you said this morning. Is there more we could do to make the world a better place? How important are the ad sales numbers being spewed at me?"

"Yeah, what you gonna do about it?"

"Follow me."

They exited the lobby and entered a vast open room full of young men staring at screens, most wearing headphones. Jordan followed Ricky all the way to the end of the space and tapped an older man on the shoulder. The man had long grey hair, wrinkled skin and a wore a plaid shirt with a plain-looking pair of black Sony headphones covering his ears. The man removed his headphones and turned around, standing up briskly as he recognized Ricky.

"Pat, this is Jordan." Ricky stated, turning to Jordan. "Pat is our principal security engineer. He spends his days outsmarting hackers around the world. Pat, Jordan here is a junkie idealist my wife picked up off the street. I think the two of you could do something interesting together.

Can you join us, Pat?" Ricky asked, nodding toward an open conference room.

Pat evaluated Jordan. After a brief pause, he smiled and nodded, rising up to follow Ricky. Once they were in the room, Ricky simply said "Nothing is off the table." then left the room and closed the door behind him.

"Lay it on me, brutha'. What's your big idea?" asked Pat, sitting comfortably in a swivel chair at the conference table.

Still standing, unsure how much freedom Ricky really intended to give him, Jordan looked at Pat hesitantly. "You ever drop acid, old man?"

"Was I a free love hippie back in the day, you mean? Yes. I never was much for the mind altering substances, but I took a hit of acid once. However, I've spent much more time studying Internet security than I ever spent tripping. Am I legit enough for you, your highness?" Pat asked, clearly uninterested in gaining approval from Jordan.

"I want to know how you feel about breaking the law. I'm not here to evaluate your coolness." Jordan responded.

"I'm not interested in getting locked up. That's why I work at Facefeed and make half as much as I could working for a hacker group. So no, I'm not comfortable breaking the law. Now are you going to answer my original question you little snot?"

Jordan paused. Sighed. He realized this was a nice gesture from Ricky, but no good would come from it. He sat down in a chair on the opposite side of the table from Pat. After a taking few breaths, he responded.

"I want to shut down the Internet. I want people to

stop being so distracted by digital technology and wake up to see how they are destroying the world around them."

"Idealist no doubt. Go on." remarked Pat.

"The world is falling apart Pat, and you're just making it worse. You sit here afraid of the law, saving Facefeed from hackers while people are rotting their brains on the cybertrash your site peddles them. Our ecosystem is literally self-destructing, compassionate community is a notion of the past, no one has time for art, for dance, for anything that is joyous in life. Instead they just get hopped up on booze, movies, and work themselves to death in the name of money, staying as distracted from reality as possible. Driving around in their air conditioned cars, sitting in their air conditioned offices. People never get a breath of fresh air, they don't even stand on their feet anymore Pat!"

Pat took a deep breath before responding. "Here we are, in the belly of the beast! Sitting in an air conditioned office of a multi-national corporation! What shall we do, Jordan? Keep going, this is great!"

"We wake them up! We end the cycle of madness. We shut down the corporations, the distractions. No more Internet is just a start. No more electricity and we will really be talking."

"How do you imagine we pull this off?"

"Smart people like you pull their heads out of their asses and use their knowledge for good. We can do this, you're the spark that could ignite a revolution, Pat."

"Or I could be the idiot who gives up a good paying job and goes to jail after being inspired by a junkie."

"I'm not a fucking junkie. I've been off dust for three

days now. I was only on that shit because I lost hope. Ann and Ricky helped me see that there is a sliver of a chance we could do something about all this. They care just as much as I do, but they're just as scared as you are about losing their material wealth and getting locked up. You see, I have nothing Pat. I've been locked up. I have nothing to lose, you have everything to lose. But we're both human, we're both alive for a limited amount of time and there's no reason why you're any better off with piles of money than I am with empty pockets. Do you want to measure your life by your wealth and comfort or by what sort of difference you can make in the world?"

Pat stopped nodding. He looked at Jordan straight-faced, beginning to take him seriously rather than simply mock him. "I've never thought about it that way." he responded after several minutes.

"Are you ready to do more than think about it? Do you want to help me?"

"I don't know yet. Why don't we try this on a small scale first? I could re-purpose some clusters and use them to grind most Internet traffic in Seattle to a halt. If I get caught, it wouldn't be that serious of a charge, and then you can see whether your brilliant scheme saves humanity."

"That's a start. How long would it take you?"

"Ah, even the criminal world wants project estimates. I don't know how fucking long it will take, Jordan. I've never done this before. How about if I just get to work and you'll know when I'm done?"

Jordan nodded and looked at Pat with sincere gratitude. His first ally. "Thank you." he said.

Pat stood up and left the conference room. Jordan returned to the lobby and asked the receptionist if he could get a lift back to Ann's office for lunch. In a few minutes the same driver with the blue BMW pulled up and whisked him back to the DEA office.

CHAPTER TWELVE

THE BRIEFING ROOM CONTAINED A large rectangular oak table surrounded with thirteen black leather swivel chairs. There was a large TV screen mounted on the far wall of the room. A digital clock indicated the time in red numbering above the door that Jordan had entered through. Ann walked in through a door on the opposite side of the room, accompanied by a woman and a man, neither of whom Jordan could recognize.

"Jordan, this is Agent Henry." Ann announced pointing to the male agent, she continued "and this is Agent Bock. After our morning debrief they showed an interest in speaking with you. Everything you say here is in strict confidence. I need to get back to my own debrief. I'll see you around four."

"Have a seat, Mr. Santarelli." Agent Bock instructed. Jordan sat down hesitantly, sweat emerging from his forehead and palms, he felt his face grow flush with unease. Being around the law had never been a good experience for him and after having just set in motion a fairly illegal operation earlier that morning his nerves were on high alert.

"What do you want to know?" he asked, always getting

a jolt of comfort and confidence when he could be the one asking the questions, but at the same time knowing full well that he was the one under questioning here.

"This Craig Ferrari guy, you purchased dust from him and accumulated about ten grand in debt?"

Now it was clear to him that his conversations with Ann were clearly not kept in confidence. Lacking the will to try and make up a facade, he responded affirmatively.

"To repay the debt, he demanded you work as an actor in his pornography business?"

Jordan nodded.

"For the record, answer the question."

"We're being recorded? Should I have a lawyer here? I want some sort of immunity guarantee!"

"You're not under arrest, you're not even under investigation. You can leave at any time, Mr. Santarelli. We have much bigger fish than you to fry here. We're speaking with you because Agent Zuckinia indicated you would like to help us."

Jordan slouched down in his chair, feeling only slightly more comfortable, he was still sweating and checking the clock every thirty seconds. After a brief pause, he responded.

"Yes, C.L. wanted me to work for him to repay the debt."

"How much was he paying you?"

"I don't know. My agent said C.L. would be keeping most of my pay anyway. And there's no way in hell I was going to go through with that shit, I'm not afraid of him. Ann said he was really after some life insurance money he could collect if I was his employee."

"Right." The agent responded, then took a deep breath and looked Jordan square in the eyes before continuing, "We need you to go back and work for him. You see, if we can catch him attempting this scheme then we can ensure he gets locked up and doesn't start another drug ring."

"Are you fucking serious? You want me to go act in porn so you can catch C.L.? What's in it for me here? Why would I do this for you? If you think I'm some do-gooder patriot like Ann, you've got the wrong guy." Jordan erupted in maniacal laughter so loud it jolted the agents back in their seats.

"If you help us, we will clear your record and offer you a scholarship to the federal academy. It's worth a lot more than your drug debt to Craig."

"He goes by C.L., you know. And no, I'm not putting my neck on the line for you. As if I wanted to become a federal agent. Forget it!"

"Well, Mr. Santarelli I'm sorry to say you don't have as many options as you might think you do. You see, we have you on record admitting to conspiring with C.L. in criminal activity."

"What?! The porn was legal and you said the dust was no big deal. I thought you had bigger fish to fry?"

"Yes, and we'll use whatever leverage we can to compel you to help us do just that."

"Are you fucking serious? I'm leaving."

As Jordan stood up Agent Henry spoke up for the first time, "We will arrest you right here, Jordan." he said, calmly but with authority.

Jordan ran out of the room, using the door he had entered through from the lobby. Once in the lobby he bounded for the stairs and began running down. No one seemed to be chasing him. He got to the ground floor and exited the building after taking a brief moment to glance up the stairs and confirm that he was not being followed. Maybe they were bluffing after all, he thought. Fucking fuzz.

He was unsure where to go next, the realization that he was now on the run from both the feds and his dealer was slowly sinking in. Jordan walked around the block and made his way toward the waterfront. He found a fairly desolate park with a dock stretching out into the Puget Sound and followed it down to the furthest distance over the water, sitting with his legs dangling over the edge above the gentle, dark blue waves below.

Ann had betrayed him. He thought she was on his side, but clearly she was more interested in helping the DEA. Ricky appeared to be willing to help him, but who knew how long it would be before Pat was able to do something, assuming he didn't just flake out. And would his brilliant plan even make a difference in the world? Wake people up to the absurdity of their corporate-driven lives?

Looking down at the reflection of his face in the waves below, Jordan saw the pain in his eyes. He was hopeless and began to feel the utter sadness that he had felt in his heart for most of his life begin to well up. He continued staring into the water, his face transfigured and in constant flux with the changing waves. Should he just give up? Take the plunge he had been too cowardice to fully commit to before? Going back to dust wasn't an option, he couldn't bear to go back to that non-existence.

He supposed he could find another job, but how

different is that meaningless existence from his life as an addict? From death? He either needed to find a way to change the world, or off himself. As he continued staring into the water, he lacked the courage to do anything more than think and look at his own reflection. The waves continued to flow, his face continued to change, each moment creating an entirely new configuration, a unique image that only held for a second and would never be replicated again. It was mesmerizing, he was transfixed by the changing image.

"Jordan, is it?" a woman asked as she sat down next to him.

Looking up, he recognized the face of the woman who had started at the coffee shop the day he was fired. He couldn't recall her name. She filled his memory gap before he had a chance to respond.

"Hannah." she announced, reaching out her hand in greeting.

"Right, Hannah. How's the new job?" Jordan asked, attempting and failing to muster some enthusiasm.

"It's been quite an interesting start, with you getting fired and then some crazy man with a gun coming in. Ali is the only reason I'm staying. You know he wanted to talk with you? Did you get his voicemail?"

"I lost my phone. Man with a gun? What?"

"I don't know. It scared the shit out of me, cops came and got him though. He was looking for you."

"Oh, well Ali was probably right to let me go. All I do is bring trouble around. You going to keep working there?"

"Yeah, I was actually just down here to buy some flowers before my shift, hoping to brighten up the store and heal its energy after yesterday's events. Want to help me pick some out? You can help carry them back to the store with me, then you can talk to Ali. I think he wants to apologize to you."

"Hah, I doubt it. But I've got nothing better to do." Jordan stood up, dusted off his pants and followed Hannah through the market picking out flowers for the coffee shop.

CHAPTER THIRTEEN

"JORDAN! YOU GOT MY MESSAGE? Hannah! You didn't give up on me? Thank God!" Ali greeted the two as they entered the shop with their hands full carrying boxes of brightly colored blossoms.

"Of course not Ali, but let's try to keep the drama down today, yeah?" Hannah answered.

"I brought these flowers to help brighten up the store and ran into Jordan while I was down at the market. I thought you two might want to talk." She nodded to a table for Jordan to set down the flowers on as she set hers down and began sorting them into colorful bottles.

Jordan looked over to Ali, uncertainly, after setting down his box.

"Come, sit, let's talk." Ali said warmly.

The two sat in the far corner of the store at a table. Jordan didn't know what to say. He wasn't even sure why he was fired, so he wasn't sure what sort of apology might get his job back for him. He decided to just start with a simple one.

"I'm sorry." He said.

"Stop. I'm the one apologizing here, Jordan. I fired you under duress, a man had threatened me and my store, I sacrificed you to save myself. It ended up doing me no good, the man came after me anyway. I learned a tough lesson. I'm sorry. I would like to offer you your job back."

Jordan sat and took in Ali's story, he was surprised by the lengths C.L. was willing to go. He was also grateful that he might now be able to add Ali to his meager list of allies. At the same time, he knew that C.L. would soon be visiting the coffee shop again looking for him.

"I've gotta go. Thanks for telling me what happened." Jordan responded with agitated gratitude before getting up and heading for the door.

"Don't go!" shouted Hannah.

Jordan stopped and looked back at her. She was beautiful. Blonde hair curling down to her shoulders shining in the sunlight that shone through the shop windows. Her bright blue eyes were filled with more hope than Jordan had ever known. She must be ignorant of the evil in the world, Jordan thought.

"Help me setup these flowers. One vase per table, plus more in the windows."

Unsure how to respond, he thought back to Ann's statement when he was ready to sail away forever. "Fight." he said under his breath. Knowing he would be found if he stayed here, if not by C.L., then by Ann, Ricky or the DEA. It must take a special kind of stupid to have both a dealer and the DEA after you, Jordan reflected. He breathed deeply, taking in Hannah's beautiful eyes, glowing sundress covered in bright pastels, and a molecule of her courage seemed to leave her soul and enter his. He nodded and took two vases to place on the table where Ali was still sitting.

Once the store was decorated customers seemed to

pour in with greater number than Jordan had ever seen before. As he worked washing dishes and keeping the front bar stocked, he began to overhear customers complaining about their phones not working.

"Facefeed is down and the Internet is painfully slow!" one remarked.

"Yeah, I know, what are we supposed to do with ourselves?" responded a young man in line behind her.

"I don't know, but I better get a refund from AV&S, this is awful!"

Jordan grinned, maybe Pat's plan was already set in motion. Or maybe the Internet was just having issues. In either case, he was getting what he wanted.

"The credit card reader's not working. Take a look, Jordan?" asked Ali handing him a customer's credit card.

More customers continued to enter the store and the queue quickly grew to the door. No one was looking at their phones, as was usually to be expected of those waiting in line, instead they were talking with each other, albeit about the fact that their phones didn't work. Jordan's smile grew broader. It was the first time he had smiled all week.

He swiped the customer's card and the reader immediately output "No Connection" on its screen. He was no tech whiz, but he knew what that message meant. He tried the card again and saw the same message appear.

"Got any cash?" he asked the customer.

They rustled around in their purse and produced a twenty dollar bill. Jordan made change and told Ali the machine was down.

"Cash only!" Ali shouted at the growing line of customers.

The store wi-fi was down, customers cell phones had no 'net connection, the credit card reader's dedicated cell connection didn't even work. Something was up. Customers continued pouring into the store and began discussing more diverse subject matter as they waited in line. Jordan pinched himself, he couldn't believe this was actually happening.

A man in a suit entered the store, bypassing the queue and approaching Jordan. Looking up, Jordan recognized the driver Ricky had sent for him earlier that day.

"Ricky sent me to pick you up. He says Pat is coming over for dinner to discuss your project and Ann wants to make an apology."

Jordan wasn't sure what to do. Ali was eyeing him and the man suspiciously. He had no interest in seeing Ann or Ricky, but the opportunity to see Pat, given the sudden turn of events, was overwhelming. He nodded and told Ali he had to go.

"Come back tomorrow?" Ali asked, with more than a sliver of frustration.

"Yes, yes definitely. I'm sorry to leave in the middle of this rush, but I have to go." he responded.

As he walked toward the door, he looked back and admired Hannah as she prepared espressos for customers with her ceaseless grace, unencumbered by the deluge of customers. He waved goodbye.

"See you!" she called out.

When he got into the blue BMW, Jordan was relieved to see that it was just the driver and him inside. No DEA agents. The car joined the evening rush of traffic on the freeway, slowly making its way across the lake to the Zuckinia residence.

CHAPTER FOURTEEN

"**A**LWAYS RUSHING OFF, I WONDER what he's up to now?" Ali appeared to be directing his query to the dumbfounded customer standing in front of him. He gave them their change as they moved to the left and waited for their warmed milk and espresso without responding. Hannah presumed the question was intended for her, and responded after a brief pause.

"He's either going to do something amazing, kill himself, or end up in jail. Maybe all three. He has something special, but it's as much of a burden as it is a gift. We can't control him, but we can support him." Hannah remarked.

"He reminds me of my younger self. Coming to America and becoming a business owner was a distant dream when I was his age. You don't have to remind me of the power of hope and hard work. Although I'm not sure he gets the hard work part." Ali commented as he continued to help the onslaught of customers.

After a few hours the store ran out of milk and change. Hannah went to the bank but their system was down so they couldn't provide any change, only accept deposits. Thankfully, the grocer was happy to offer milk on credit and had some extra change he was willing to provide as well.

Back at the store, keeping up with demand continued to be a struggle and by the end of the day both Ali and Hannah were exhausted, there was hardly a coffee bean left in the shop and they had made more revenue than they had ever collected in a single day.

"This Internet problem seems good for business. Who would have thought?" remarked Ali as the two walked from the store to drop-off the deposit at the bank after closing up.

"So much hard work and energy goes into building Internet technology, yet it seems to cause more harm than good to our society. Companies like Facefeed are just profiting from the distraction they create." Hannah remarked.

"And so all anyone wants is to stare at their phone all day."

"Most people seem content with it."

"Most people in this city pay their rent by working for the companies that make these distractions. In fact it's probably a good part Facefeed money in this bag right here. There's no simple answer."

There was a queue at the night deposit, other business owners seemed to be making unprecedented deposits as well.

"Good day, eh?" one remarked as Ali and Hannah approached.

"Indeed, more people out and about with the Internet down."

"Tomorrow might be different, most ATMs are down and people's cash supplies will be dwindling."

"Oh, I'm sure the Internet will be back before we get home. Just some glitch, yeah?"

The man who had queued behind them chimed in.

"It's not so simple. I hear the Internet Exchange downtown has been burnt to the ground. Server soup the nerds called it. Apparently the Conblast data center in Bellevue burnt down too."

"Wow, sounds like some serious arson. How do we get money from the bank if the Internet stays offline? Surely they don't exclusively rely on it for their operation?" Ali responded with alarm.

The man shrugged, unknowingly.

After parting ways, Hannah returned home and saw several missed calls on her cell phone. She dialed her Mom first. The cellular voice network seemed to still be in operation.

"Hannah? Our Internet's not working, can you come over and take a look?"

"Mom, I don't know any more about that stuff than you do. And besides, it's down for everyone. Apparently someone burned down the network."

"You can't just burn down the Internet! You've been filling your head with rubbish. The TV isn't working either."

"The TV comes over the Internet now, Mom. Why don't you and Dad do something different for a change, I don't know, talk with each other? Go for a walk?"

"Now, now. You don't have to be mean, if you don't want to help your parents than just say so."

"I'm coming over, but don't expect me to fix anything."

The amount her parents, and the rest of society for that matter, depended on the Internet was baffling to Hannah. She never really found much use for it and hardly ever even used her phone, nor did she own or desire a television. Being out and about, exploring, creating and sharing took up all the free time she had. These activities also cost much less money and used hardly any electricity.

Upon arriving at her parents house, Hannah saw a note on the front door, it read: "Went next door, their TV works!"

She shrugged and walked to the neighbors house who had lived next door to Hannah's parents for over twenty years, as far back as she could remember.

The neighbors greeted her warmly, but had a panicked look on their face.

"We've got an antenna!" they announced. As Hannah entered the living room she saw her parents sitting in front of the screen where a woman in a red blazer was talking.

"The biggest cyber attack in history struck Seattle today, bringing Internet service to a halt and disrupting the business and personal lives of all area residents." the news woman announced with a look of terror on her face.

"Bullshit!" Hannah commented resentfully.

Everyone looked at her questioningly, appearing to side with the woman on TV.

"We had more business at the coffee shop today than ever before!" she announced loudly, competing for attention with the reporter on the screen.

"Well, that's nice hon, but the rest of us, you know, with real jobs, are not able to get anything done without the Internet."

"How real is your job if it depends entirely on the Internet?"

"Real enough to put a roof over your head and food on your plate." her father responded.

Her Dad worked for a cloud sales company, his business depended entirely on the Internet and Hannah was tech-versed enough to understand that. However, it still struck her that so much money could be made off of so little actual, real, physical work.

"Why is your time spent…using the Internet, apparently…worth so much more money than my time making coffee?"

"Because before Saleswad existed companies had to hire far more people to track and manage their sales. Now we automate all of that for them, and save them a lot of money."

"Oh, I get it. You make more money if you destroy more jobs. If I could invent a machine to make coffee without having to hire baristas, for less money than it costs to hire a barista, and do it at a profit, I would be rich."

"Exactly. Automation is the miracle of Capitalism. That's a great idea Hannah, you should do it! It would be so much more productive than your art projects!" her father commented.

Hannah was enraged by the remark, her parents clearly showing how their values differed from her own. Their righteous laughter poured salt in her wounds and drove her to depart without saying another word.

CHAPTER FIFTEEN

J ORDAN WAS SO EXCITED TO see Pat as he entered the Zuckinia mansion he began asking questions before anyone else could get a word out.

"What happened? Was this all you? I didn't realize it would involve arson, man! I could have done that, I thought you were doing some sort of hacker shit."

"It was hacker arson, Jordan." Pat responded.

"Have a seat, look at this salmon!" Ricky commented, pointing to a beautiful fillet on the table.

Ann was sitting silently at the table. Jordan looked at her questioningly, "What the fuck was with the questioning? Now the DEA is after me? I thought you wanted to help me."

"Just sit down and eat, Jordan. We have a lot to discuss." Ricky stated, attempting to take charge.

"Does your Internet work here?" Jordan asked.

"No, just eat, won't you?"

Jordan looked around the table suspiciously to ensure the others were eating too, but his paranoia was unwarranted as he saw everyone digging into the salmon. He was hungry himself, but more hungry for answers. After taking a few bites he set down his fork and resumed the questioning.

"What did you do, Pat? I can't wait any longer."

"I am interested too, what did you do?" Ricky asked Pat.

"Remember those centrifuges in Iran that mysteriously spun themselves into oblivion? It was a cyber attack by the CIA. I basically used the same concept to burn up the servers at the Internet Exchange downtown and at a few Conblast data centers." Pat explained, seeming to be more interested in the salmon than the discussion.

"No way! That's sick. How long will it last?" Jordan asked.

"You didn't use any company hardware for this stunt did you?" Ricky interrupted.

"Of course I did, you were the one who asked me to do it and said everything was on the table."

"Lies! I asked you to talk with Jordan, bounce some ideas around, that's all. Just because everything is on the table doesn't mean to act without even informing me of what you plan on doing."

"So everything wasn't on the table?" Jordan asked.

"Everything within reason was. There has to be a way we could have done this without causing permanent harm, without burning shit down. Now we're criminally liable. I have to call our lawyers."

"What exactly could we have done without breaking any laws?" Pat asked.

"You know, slow the site down, collaborate with some other sites to promote a Day of Disconnection or something."

"A publicity stunt? That's what you wanted. That's not the way Jordan here was talking."

"I didn't want a fucking publicity stunt and you know it, Ricky. Pat did some legit shit. This is the first time I've gotten any traction and it's working great." Jordan interjected.

Ann jumped into the quickly escalating argument, "You're not on the right side of the law, Jordan. Your dealings with Craig Ferrari are not going to get you in any trouble, but this Internet stuff is going to get you locked up. I can't hear about it. I'm sorry for the way my agents treated you today, they were out of bounds, but now you're legitimately breaking the law. I don't want you to rope my husband and his company into any more of your revolution crap. You can stay the night, but you should find another place to stay tomorrow."

"Fuck you. What about my soul-spark and all the other hippy bullshit you and Ricky were spewing? You want to save the world? My ass. You just want to make money and live your upper-crust lifestyle like everyone else in the 1%. You're either full of shit or the biggest hypocrites on Earth." Jordan yelled, standing up and beginning to shake with anger.

"The kid's right." Pat joined in. "You're only willing to do things that don't jeopardize your wealth to make the world a better place, you might as well do nothing at all. You're causing more harm than good, and you will continue to do so as long as you're more interested in gaining wealth than making the world a better place. You can spew all the corporate responsibility bullshit you want, but the truth is you just want to make as much money as you can and will do as little as is required to serve humanity so long as it keeps the customers coming."

"You're fired Pat. You're wrong and you're fired and I'm sick of both of you." Ricky was yelling now, entering a rage, "Get out of my fucking house. I need to call my lawyers."

Ann was the only one still sitting, the disgusted expression on her face said it all.

"Fuck it, let's go." Pat said to Jordan as he got up and headed toward the door.

Jordan followed Pat to his car, a silver Porsche parked in the driveway. Sitting in the front seat he thought about whether Pat was legit, or if he would clam up and beg Ricky for his job tomorrow. All he knew for sure was that Ann and Ricky were no longer his allies, they never really were in the first place. Just do-gooders with no backbone.

"I want to show you something, Jordan." Pat said as they merged onto the highway. He slammed on the gas and got the car going 90 in a matter of seconds.

Jordan remained silent, thinking about what might come down with Ricky and his legal team. How did people live without either being under the thumb of the government or a criminal organization? He couldn't remember the last time he was free to just be.

As they sped down the highway, Pat got the Porsche up to 160, the Seattle skyline quickly came within sight. After a few more minutes they were off the freeway and idling in front of an unmarked building near Lake Union.

"This is an NSA office. I have a friend who works here. Hang on." Pat whispered before stepping out of the car.

Pat walked up to a door on the side of the building. He stood still and didn't knock or ring a bell. A few seconds passed by and then a man walked out of the door. The two greeted each other with a warm embrace and Pat led the man back to his car.

"Jordan, meet Rob. Rob, meet Jordan, the kid with bigger balls than we ever had back in our revolutionary days. Remember how we used to talk about using the 'net to bring back democracy? I tell you, this kid takes it to the next level."

"You two didn't have anything to do with the attack today, did you?"

"Attack? Who got hurt?"

"Millions of dollars in servers burnt to a crisp. Homeland is all over it."

"Huh. Let's get a drink."

Driving at a crisp 70 miles per hour along Lake Union, the three arrived at a bar on the north side of the lake in short order. Walking in and grabbing a table in the back, Pat ordered a round of brews from the bartender.

"Remember back when we really wanted to shake things up? What derailed us?" Pat asked.

"We did shake things up! You run security for the largest social network in the world and I work for the largest security agency in the world. I don't know about you, but I am proud of what I am doing for society."

"We wanted to make the world a better place, Rob. Are we doing that?"

"I don't know about better, but safer for sure. Isn't safer better? You have no idea how many times per day the banks are hacked. If it wasn't for us there would be no banking system, and the Internet would be down more days than it is up."

"But have we fixed any of the problems that bugged

us as kids? Or did we just become part of the problem without even knowing it?"

"Are you kidding me?" Jordan asked with baffled laughter. "C'mon guys, you know you're just corporate and government hags. It's obvious. You're sell outs. How are your beach houses?" Jordan remarked before taking a deep swig from his glass.

"Our beach houses have nothing on the palaces owned by the thugs we're fighting, I'll tell you that, J-Rock. Can I call you J-Rock?" asked Rob.

"No, my name is Jordan. Is my point really that hard for you to see? What makes the world a better place in your opinion, Robby-Bobby?"

"Fuck you, fine, Jordan. The world is basically fucked, that is a certainty that only the young even bother questioning. I'm just trying to keep people safe and stop things from getting worse."

"It's all about money, Rob. Don't you see that? The only thing you're keeping safe is our money. And what are you willing to sacrifice to keep people's wealth, property, money 'safe?' Spy on every phone call and e-mail? Let giant corporations run the government so they can continue increasing their wealth and expanding their power? You're not making every day people any safer or more prosperous. You're just a hired gun for people like Ricky."

"What more can I do? You think the fuckheads who took down the 'net are making the world better? Watch how our economy falls apart in a matter of days."

"Exactly! Don't you see? You mistake the health of our economy for the health of our people."

An elderly gentleman sitting alone at the table next to them looked over and said "You're both wrong. You're both right. The world is perfect."

The man appeared to have walked straight of a fairytale. His long hair was white with age, and he had a beard to match. Completing the ensemble, the man wore a thick, worn cloak.

Jordan was the first to respond, "Poetry. That never fixed anything either."

"There's nothing that needs fixing, don't you see that?" the man responded.

He stood up and approached the empty seat at their table. "I'm William, mind if I join you?"

The three shrugged and nodded, providing an uncertain affirmation.

"William Jeffrey. A poet, indeed. I teach poetry at the city college and write for a few small publications you've never heard of."

"Are you going to explain your babble or continue to spew illogical phrases?"

"Sit and listen to the wind blow with me. Stop talking and listen."

The three sat in silence for several seconds. But Jordan couldn't help himself "We're inside you idiot, there is no wind."

"Listen!" William shouted.

The three sat for a whole minute without making a sound. Then the air conditioner kicked off and the room became slightly quieter. The three nodded in bemused acknowledgement.

"You didn't notice until it stopped, did you?" William asserted.

Jordan continued to sit in silent observation. Folks sitting around other tables continued their conversations without regard for whether the air conditioner was blowing or not, their chatter provided incomprehensible background noise as the four men sat in silence. Glasses chinked, footsteps wandered, the room felt slightly warmer than it did a few moments earlier. William took a sip from his glass and set it back down, slowly moving his gaze around the table, pausing for a few seconds as he locked eyes with each of the other men before he continued.

"You have an image in your mind of the perfect world, the way things should be. Each of you have your own image, however similar they may be, the similarities create your friendship, but the images are not the same and discovering the dissimilarities could put your relationships on rocky ground. Now those women over there, with the Gucci and Prada, what do you think their perfect world looks like? If the grand universe moved closer to your perfect world, would it be closer or further from perfection for them? Or if it moved in the other direction, toward their perfection, would you be even more distraught than you already are? The universe is standing stretched in a perfect balance. This is as close to perfection as it can be."

"So no one gets what they want and the only happy people are the poets who laugh at everyone else?"

"Everyone gets what they want, they just need to find their tribe. You men seem to be questioning your current tribal membership, perhaps there is another tribe better suited for you?"

Jordan wasn't buying any of this nonsense. "Alright Gandalf, thanks for your pearls of wisdom." He responded in irritation, continuing, "You make it sound so simple. But I can't just standby while I see the world going to hell, what's the point of that?"

"Suit yourself, but the more you try to play God the more the real master of the universe will show you how powerless you are. When you surrender is up to you, but I reckon you'll be feeling only more pain as you march down this revolutionary road of yours."

With that, William stood up, leaving his beer on the table. He wandered out of the pub's open doorway and into the street, his grey cloak illuminated with a tinge of orange by the streetlamp.

Rob, Pat and Jordan resumed drinking their brews and looked at each other in silence. Jordan's only reason for living was to fight back against corruption and injustice. He certainly sought to find his tribe, but only so that they could work together toward a more just world. Looking back at Rob he felt it was foolish to keep him in the dark any longer, if he was going to help the cause he needed to know that they were serious.

"We are the ones who shut off the Internet, Rob. Pat did the handy work. Do you want to turn us in or do you want to stop being such a hypocrite and join us?"

"Fuck!" Pat burst out, slamming his first on the table and glaring at Jordan. "You can't just announce shit like that."

Rob stood up and exited the pub without saying a word. Pat yelled after him but was ineffective in preventing his friend's departure.

CHAPTER SIXTEEN

H ANNAH AWOKE AT 3 AM WITH her eyes wide open and alert staring at the ceiling above her bed. She had painted the entire ceiling of her bedroom with a re-creation of Starry Night when she first moved into her flat. Sitting up and looking around her room she saw three re-sealed buckets of red paint she had leftover from a canceled commission last month. She grabbed a dress out of her closet, unable to make out exactly which one it was in the darkness. After putting on her dress and then sitting down to pull on some stockings, she darted out of her bedroom with the cans of paint stacked on top of each other in her arms.

Silently making her way downstairs to the entryway, she slipped on some shoes and exited the apartment as silently as possible. Loading up her car with the paint and starting the engine, she turned on her headlights and drove toward the coffee shop.

She arrived around 4am, the street was empty, silent and dark. The sidewalk was illuminated by glowing yellow street lamps overhead. Parking directly in front of the store, she unlocked the entrance and brought in the paint cans. Locking the door behind her, she turned on all of the lights and began to play a Jimi Hendrix mix on the store sound system.

Realizing she had failed to bring a paintbrush or any other painting supplies, she looked around the store to find something that would work. She used a knife to wedge the paint cans open and found a cloth that would have to make due for a paintbrush. As guitar riffs wailed from the speakers she looked at the blank white walls and prayed for inspiration. Upon opening her eyes the first thing she noticed was the flowers she had put throughout the store with Jordan the previous day. She thought of the poor soul and his struggle, his failure to see the beauty in life. She looked up at the blank walls and began to paint a stem with the only color available to her.

Time flew by. As the sun rose the store was filled with sunlight. Hannah's creations looked even bolder and brighter than when she had laid down the paint. The lock on the front door clicked open and the door chimed as Ali entered.

"It's beautiful, Hannah! You are bringing the store to life. Thank you!" Ali shouted over the opening chords of All Along the Watchtower playing on the speakers overhead.

Hannah dropped her makeshift paintbrush in surprise at Ali's sudden arrival. She was standing on top of a table with a can of paint at her side, the rag she had been using to paint swelled with a red stain circling around it on the floor.

"I know I should have asked, Ali. I was just inspired and had to get it out. I was sick of the white walls."

"It's perfect. We need to open the store now though, it's 6:30!"

Hannah gasped. "Already? Wow! Let me move my car."

Five seconds after Hannah departed the store, Jordan entered.

"Ali! Were you able to get any change from the bank?"

"I got $100 in change, they are rationing funds with the Internet outage. We will be okay. If people don't have cash and want to barter let me know. We might be better off going that way than relying on cash."

Jordan looked up toward the heavens with gratitude, it was the closest he ever got to praying. He made a double take after seeing that the ceiling was no longer a blank, pale white. There was an image of a man's face painted on the ceiling, leaves growing from his head and only a giant heart in place of a torso. His gaze turned to the surrounding walls, painted with flowers and vines, all bright red in color. The art glistened in the sunlight, the paint was still drying.

"Hannah's been busy, eh?"

"Beautiful, isn't it? You bring the thugs, she brings the light. The store is back in balance."

Jordan sighed. "I'm sorry, Ali. I never meant for my personal business to come here."

"It was out of your control. Now, if you're really sorry then help me get the store ready."

Business was surprisingly slow after the unexpected uptick the previous day. A few of the elderly and other unemployed regulars popped in, but the morning rush was completely absent.

"Where is everyone?" Ali asked.

"Hard to tell with the 'net still down, no Facebook or Reddit to check." Jordan commented with a smirk.

"Go scout it out the old fashioned way, Jordan, figure out what's going on!" Ali ordered, a bit dismayed.

Jordan walked out of the store and down the street, observing empty busses and sparse sidewalks. He began walking toward downtown and was surprised by how desolate the city was.

A man in a suit walked past Jordan in the opposite direction ranting "I better still get paid!"

Jordan turned around and chased after the suited man. "Hey! What's going on?"

"Office is closed, 'net is still down and we can't get any work done."

"Party time!" Jordan responded. "Cup of coffee?"

The man shook his head and speeded up to gain distance from Jordan. Mumbling under his breath and stomping with a heated step.

Jordan entered the financial district and saw all the buildings were closed, many with explanatory notes posted on the doors, others simply with large signs reading "CLOSED." He began walking back toward the coffee shop, but a Jeep pulled up along side him and a familiar voice shouted "Jordan! Get in!"

"I'm working today, fuck off man." Jordan responded, looking up to see Rob leaning out the window. He regretted divulging his actions at the pub the previous night and Rob's response suggested that the two would not be working together.

"You gonna arrest me?"

"No man, but the FBI is on the hunt hardcore today. Get in."

Jordan considered the undesirable possibility of being

arrested by the FBI and compared it with getting in Rob's Jeep, then opted for the lesser of two evils.

"I have to go back to work." he said as he got into the passenger seat of the Jeep.

"You can't just shut down the Internet for an entire city and expect to carry on as usual."

"Why not?"

"You could get locked up for decades man, don't you get it? You're a terrorist."

"Fuck this country."

"Listen, I'm trying to help you."

Jordan interrupted him, "You want to help me, Rob? Or are you 'just trying' to help? I'm sick of pussy-assed motherfucking hypocritical cowards like you thinking you're saving the world while you destroy it. Cuz' if you really want to help, then say so. But listen to me for fuck's sake. If you want to 'save me' then fuck off and let me out."

"Damn, kid. Calm down. I could be arrested for picking you up and not turning you in, knowing what I know. What more proof do you need that I'm on your side here?"

"Just take me up to the coffee shop."

"You've got it, but we need to talk. People are freaking out that they won't get paid, businesses are virtually shut down, do you realize how much havoc you caused?"

"I'm only getting started, Rob. Are you in to go all the way, or are you trying to talk me down?"

"How is this a better fucking world, Jordan? Everyone is freaking the fuck out. Are you so much happier now that Facebook doesn't work?"

The Jeep pulled to a stop in front of the coffee shop,

Jordan opened the passenger door and paused, looking back at Rob.

"Tonight the power goes. Do you want to help?"

Rob sighed, shaking his head. "I'm not turning you in, but I'm not helping you either."

"Revolutions don't happen without shaking things up. This is the most non-violent revolution in history and you're still not willing to accept the small price for a better world."

Jordan shut the door behind him and returned to the shop. Rob stayed parked out in front, with the engine idling. Walking into the store, Jordan saw that it was still virtually empty.

"Businesses are all closed downtown, apparently people are panicked that they won't have their jobs with the 'net down." Jordan informed his two colleagues.

"So people are all just sitting at home worrying about their jobs? That's not how I envisioned things going when Capitalism came to an end." Hannah remarked, laughing.

A woman walked in with a tiny black dog on a leash, as she ordered a latte the dog wandered to the extent that the leash would allow, sniffing out the unfamiliar surroundings. Paying with cash, she walked over to the espresso bar to wait for her drink. The dog continued sniffing around a nearby table. The woman wore a long red dress and admired the art on the surrounding walls. Removing her sunglasses she commented to the barista "It's beautiful!"

The woman's cell phone rang. She reached in her black leather purse to grab the phone and answer it. "Back on, yeah? I'll be down in fifteen." she clicked the phone off and returned it to her purse. As Hannah put her completed latte on the bar, with a swirling foam rose on top, the woman took the drink and commented "Net's back up!" as she turned to exit the shop.

"Well, thank goodness for that!" Ali commented, taking down the 'cash only' sign from the door.

Jordan saw Rob sitting outside in his jeep, talking on his cell phone. Nervous about possibly getting turned in and confused as to where the man actually stood on all of this, he told Ali he had to go but would be back.

CHAPTER SEVENTEEN

"THE INTERNET IS BACK UP. That didn't take long." Jordan said with surprise and disgust as he got back into the passenger seat of Rob's Jeep.

Rob didn't respond. Jordan looked over at him cautiously to see if it was possible to glean any insight into his thinking from his facial expression, but Rob's face was a stone wall, expressionless, lips shut tight with neither a frown nor a smile present. He started the engine and drove the Jeep back onto the street, making a U-turn and heading down the road toward the highway.

"We're leaving today. Pat, you and me are all targets now and it won't be long before our window out of the country closes."

"Power first."

"You're crazy, kid. The power grid is a lot more secure than the Internet. There is no hack like the one Pat pulled off that will bring it down."

"People need to see how they are destroying themselves and the planet. It will only happen if we disrupt their lives, disconnect the grid and reconnect humanity."

"That's all well and good, but why is it our job to do that? You want to free the people you need to have them join you willingly. Right now you just sound like some raging lunatic dictator."

"They will join willingly when they see the true potential for change. If we work together, the government and corporations will be powerless over us. We are the blood in their machines and we have the ability to change the direction of our society. Everyone has given up hope because they know that one individual can't do anything significant. Once we throw a wrench in the gear work of Capitalism, it will give people the opportunity to re-calibrate, see their power, and then they will join willingly."

"Like they re-calibrated with the Internet outage? I think that they'll be asking for your head on a pike when they find out you were responsible. You just don't get it, we need to go if you don't want to end up in a penitentiary."

The Jeep pulled on to the interstate highway heading south toward the airport. Jordan was not content with Rob's escape plan. Leaving the country after only bringing the Internet down for a few days seemed ridiculous to him. Surely he could do more before fleeing. Fleeing was never in his plan, he gave up on fleeing when he was on the boat with Ann.

"I'm not running, Rob. Stop the car and let me out, then you can get on your jet and I won't stop you."

Rob sighed, looked over at Jordan and pulled to the shoulder, gesturing for him to get out without a word.

Jordan looked back at Rob before closing the door, "You sure you don't want to really make a change before you run away? Where are you going anyway?"

"Copenhagen." Rob said as he pulled away, the passenger door slamming itself shut with the car's propulsion.

Jordan looked around, he was standing in the shoulder of the highway and not sure how to get back to the coffee shop. He started walking with the flow of traffic, wondering how far away the next exit was. He watched all the cars rushing by on his left, each emitting a bit more CO_2 into the atmosphere, each driver mindlessly going about their business. How could people know the world is coming to an end and still continue destroying it, with a smile on their face none the less? He briefly considered diving into the oncoming traffic, desperate to get people to wake up. Or was he just entertaining an inner death wish? An inner hopelessness? Continuing down the highway he saw an exit ahead and began jogging toward it.

As he began jogging down the offramp, a car slowed down along side him as the passenger window began to roll down. Pat was yelling at him from the rolled down window. "Jordan! Get in, I'll help you."

Looking over, he saw the earnestness in Pat's expression. This was the man who gave up his high paying corporate gig and actually did something for the cause. This was the only person Jordan felt he could truly trust. Jordan got in the car.

"Shutting down the power is a manual job, that makes it hard, but it also means you can do some of the work this time."

Jordan saw the back seat of Pat's car was full of gasoline jugs, the smell was awful. "What are we doing?"

"Think molotov cocktails. The easiest way to shut down a substation is triggering its fire suppression system."

As the car pulled up to a power substation south of the ballpark, Pat got out and grabbed one of the containers from the back seat. He stuffed a rag into the nozzle and lit it, then used both hands to toss the container into the substation. Finally, he ran back to the car and drove off before it was clear anything had happened, Jordan was in shock. He always thought more planning would be involved, this was all happening so fast he wasn't sure what to do.

"How many substations are in the city?"

"Dozens. We will not get all of them. The Internet outage, the power outage, how do you expect people to know it was you, to know your intention here?" Pat responded.

An explosion suddenly sounded from behind them, it was so loud the car shook. Jordan looked back and saw sparks flying in all directions from the substation as a fire broke out in one corner near where Pat had chucked the gasoline canister. The lights of the buildings around them flickered off, the stoplight ahead of them went from red to nothingness. Pat turned right.

"Fuck! That was loud." Jordan remarked, stunned.

"It will take the utilities about half an hour to call the police. We need to be out of the city by then and on our way to the airport. Now what's your plan to get the message out?"

"I don't want to leave a message, Pat. If I have to explain myself, then what's the point? I want people to figure this out for themselves, I'm just starting the conversation, the train of thought. It will be much more powerful if they realize it organically. But shutting off the system for a day or two, that won't cut it. They rebuild too fast."

"Permanent damage is impossible, you can't stop

things that easily, Jordan. You would need an army. Right now you're just a menace that society wants locked up. How do you think this will be any different than the Internet outage?"

As they pulled up near the city college, Jordan saw the wizard walking by. "William!" he called out, grabbing the elderly man's attention.

"Terrorist!" the man responded warmly, walking up to the car.

Seeing the jugs of gasoline in the back and covering his nose, William continued "You're out of your mind, how much suffering do you want to bring on yourself?"

"Jordan!" came a woman's voice, looking around Jordan saw Hannah running up toward the car.

"What are you doing?!" she shouted.

"Fixing the world, Hannah. We really need to get going."

"Stop it. You're being a fool, Jordan. How are you going to save the world while you're behind bars?"

"All great revolutionaries spend time behind bars."

"For demanding justice, Jordan. Not for attacking their own country. You'll go to jail with people cheering for the police, not for you."

William nodded. "She's right, kid."

Jordan was so angry he couldn't speak. He began pressing his fist into the dashboard of the car, trying to find the words to communicate some sort of understanding to all of the people around him. No matter how hard he tried, no one seemed to understand him.

"Just get out of the car and breathe for a minute, hon." Hannah said, opening the passenger door.

Jordan stepped out and stood with William and Hannah.

"No time!" Pat said, as he suddenly sped off. Jordan nearly fell as the car suddenly departed.

The three stood and watched as Pat pulled up to a substation two blocks away and hurled another red gasoline container into the fenced off electrical works.

"Do you think he's doing things for the same reason as you, Jordan?" William asked. "Remember you each have a different ideal, do you think he wants the social enlightenment you're after?"

"He left his job for me, he shut down the Internet for me, and now he's shutting down the power grid for me. Of course he has the same ideal as I do."

"He did those things for you, eh? How do you know that?"

"I recruited him, he was just another working stiff at Facefeed before I talked him into changing the world."

A gunshot rang out in unison with an explosion from the substation where Pat was, fire and sparks were blazing as more lights flashed off from surrounding buildings. Jordan saw Pat laying on the pavement, blood running from his head.

The three ran to see what had just happened. Pat's arm was outstretched with a pistol clasped in his hand. Jordan looked around, running around the scene trying to find a clue to suggest that something other than what was obvious had just happened. Despite all the clamor, no police were in sight and no sirens could be heard. As Jordan returned to Pat's body, lying motionless on the pavement, the signs of suicide were abundantly clear. Pat had killed himself.

A second explosion suddenly sounded from within the substation, sparks flew everywhere and a giant fire erupted.

As Jordan struggled to wake Pat up, desperate to save his life, he saw a note folded in Pat's hand. He reached down and removed it, then unfolded the small piece of paper and recited the lone sentence scrawled inside: "There is no hope."

CHAPTER EIGHTEEN

ORDAN'S KNEES FELL OUT FROM under him and his body collapsed to the ground. His hands broke his fall and he stared over at Pat's corpse in shock, feeling as if the gunshot had simultaneously taken Pat's life and a chunk out of his own soul. Tears began rolling down his cheek. He couldn't understand why Pat had taken his own life. Trembling, his arms becoming rubber, Jordan ran his hands over the gravel beneath him. His tears grew thicker and Jordan began sobbing uncontrollably, his mouth sputtering laments and confusion.

"You don't have to understand, Jordan. Some things don't have an explanation." Hannah said, standing beside Jordan as she crouched down to console him. The calm, soothing voice came as a morsel of relief to Jordan's internal panic. He looked up at Hannah, utterly helpless.

"There is no hope? How can he think that while helping me start the revolution?" Jordan asked, not expecting an answer.

"How long have you known this man?" William asked with concern.

Blood emerged from Jordan's hands as he continued to rub them back and forth over the pavement. He pushed himself up, sitting on his knees, examining the damage he had inflicted on his palms. Then he looked over to William, considerings the man's question.

Finally, Jordan managed to put some words together and respond to William's question, "A few days, but he understood me, William. He was the only one who got it and was willing to do something about it. He was like my brother."

"Come with me, Jordan. This is no place to be. The substation is ablaze and the man who ignited it lays dead before you. Police are surely on the way."

Jordan followed William, who had been riding on a bicycle that he now walked down the sidewalk beside him. Hannah accompanied them, offering Jordan a supportive shoulder as he struggled to stay standing, his legs quivering and tears continuing to roll down his face. He walked in silence, observing those around him, still holding Pat's note rolled up in his hand.

After nearly an hour walking through the city the three arrived at a small row house near the former industrial zone that had been taken over by the tech companies. Jordan's tear ducts finally shut off as they approached the front door of Pat's house, his entire body ached, his head was spinning amidst a whirlwind of thoughts and questions.

Entering the house, William sat his bicycle outside the entrance and led the three into his living room, gesturing for them to take a seat.

"We didn't meet by accident. I'm glad we met when we did. You're struggle is more than any one soul can bear, Jordan. There are many thousands of us around the world fighting it every day. Healing the world is no easy task, it spans lifetimes."

Jordan gazed into William's eyes, desperate for an answer, a solution, an explanation. "I thought the world was perfect?"

"It is, but that doesn't mean that perfection is static. The world is constantly changing as the thoughts and actions of people change, it reflects a global conscious. It's only the world's imperfection that makes it perfect. Every person I can inspire, I can show love toward, that is how I heal myself and the world. The more love, the more connectedness, the better things will get. That's what I believe."

"That's a hopeless battle. There are people actively trying to destroy the world, some doing it intentionally, others unintentionally but doing harm none the less. If I show them love, they'll just keep doing what they do and laugh at my weakness."

"How do you know all this? It sounds like you have everything figured out, and I think that's what puts you in such a sorry state of mind. How can you possibly know what people think or what they will do? It's not possible, and assuming you do know the answer only reinforces you're negative conclusions."

Jordan sat silent, rubbing his ravaged hands together and considering what William was saying. He wasn't convinced, but he had to admit that his plan was not working out as he had hoped, certainly not the way he was convinced it would if he put it into action.

"You've spent so long living in hatred, Jordan. Why not try using love and seeing what happens?" Hannah said, in her calm, warm and caring voice. Her blue eyes wide open, lips pursed, Jordan had never seen someone with so much love in their heart.

"How can you not be angry when you know about all the corruption? All the pollution? All the greed and selfishness? How could love possibly bring any of these to an end? Disruption is the only way." Jordan responded.

"Maybe these people you think are evil are just sick, Jordan. Maybe they are unloved. Maybe they have constantly been attacked and you're just another foe trying to hurt them? What do you expect from them?" Hannah looked at him almost in horror, surprised that this was not obvious to Jordan.

Jordan couldn't respond, the horror of Pat's death still blowing craters in his mind. William grunted. "How about something to eat?" he asked, breaking the silence.

Jordan nodded, laying back into his seat and staring transfixed into Hannah's eyes. William stood up and wandered into the kitchen. Moments later, the sizzle of the skillet and the smell of cooking meat ignited a hunger in Jordan he had not felt since departing Ann's mansion. As he began to salivate, he looked around the living room, admiring the simple homeliness William had created with mismatched, worn furniture, wooden boards lining the ceiling and a painting of the French riviera hanging across the living room from where he was sitting. The green faded rug in the center of the living room was covered by a large marble coffee table, atop which were photos of William with his wife and kids, all smiling as they posed in front of landmarks throughout Europe. His gaze returned to Hannah and her unanswered question.

"I don't know. I don't think I have it in me. I don't know how to be a kind and loving type of person, it comes so easily to you as if its in your nature, it is not that way for me."

"I learned it the same way as you will, if you want to learn. There is no inherent nature, Jordan. We are only the result of our decisions, our attitudes and what we have learned from experience. All you need to do is have some willingness."

Jordan reflected over the years he had spent thinking about how much better things would be when people saw things his way. He felt utterly heartbroken to have finally taken action and failed so miserably. He shook his head, staring down at the rug. Thinking about his trouble with C.L., the DEA, and the FBI investigating the Internet outage he had planned. And now the power failures at two substations in the city. It all seemed minuscule compared with the loss of Pat, his brother in arms.

"Look at each person walking by." Hannah said, pointing out the window. "Think about something beautiful in them, try to see the good, Jordan. Try it now."

Jordan followed her instructions, seeing two young men, work badges dangling from the lanyards around their necks. His first thought sounded loudly in his mind, "Fucking tech zombies." He shook his head and tried desperately to see their inner beauty. Jordan noticed their smiles and the shiny silver watch one was wearing around his wrist.

Hannah leaned forward and nodded questioningly at Jordan.

"They are smiling, they must be happy. And that's a nice watch." The words feebly slipping from his lips.

"We all start somewhere. See? Maybe they're not evil?"

"Maybe."

"Dinner is ready!" came William's voice from the kitchen.

Jordan rose eagerly, his stomach grumbling with hunger as he entered the dining room and saw the magnificent feast laid out before them.

"Wow, thank you William, this looks wonderful!" Hannah said as she sat down across from Jordan.

Jordan nodded in agreement, looking over to William and saying "Thank you."

"Cooking for others brings me great joy, dig in! Let's sit our problems aside for a moment and enjoy."

A banjo strumming bluegrass could be heard from a speaker in the kitchen and was soon joined by a passionate harmonica. Jordan took a bite of the steak on his plate and felt his worries fade into the background. He looked around the table, at Hannah, William, the warm food, and savored the moment. He felt like things might be okay, even if he didn't fix all the world's problems. For the moment, he felt content. He had hardly a dollar to his name and was probably homeless, but for once he felt loved.

CHAPTER NINETEEN

"**Y**OU CAN STAY HERE TONIGHT, Jordan. If you need a place to stay." William said as he took his plate into the kitchen.

"I've got a place, it's just, uh, I'm not sure how safe it is right now." Jordan stood up, taking his plate and following William into the kitchen. "I'll do the dishes."

"I'm heading home. See you at the shop tomorrow, Jordan?" Hannah said, handing him her plate.

"Yeah, I'll be there."

After the dishes were washed and Hannah had departed, William invited Jordan for a smoke on his back patio.

"You going to keep at this revolution thing or are you ready to stop digging?"

"I've run out of ideas, but I have a lot of trouble to deal with. My dealer is after me, and the FBI now too it sounds like."

"That might be more pertinent than your revolution."

"I didn't think any of it would matter after I started the revolution. I thought Pat and I would change the world."

"You did, you brought the Internet down for a few days and briefly killed the power in a few neighborhoods. You stopped business for a few days, you scared a lot of people. Maybe it just wasn't the change you were hoping for?"

"I wanted people to stop destroying the planet, stop feeding their souls to the machine."

"The machine is history, Jordan. You can't stop it, no one ever has. History marches on no matter what."

"If we started from a clean slate we could make such a better society, it's so clear, so obvious."

"That's a nice fantasy, but that's all it is."

"So I just spread love, inspire a few souls? That's it? What's the point?"

"It's not much, but its infinitely more than you could do if you were dead, or in jail."

Jordan nodded, taking a hit from the pipe William was sharing with him. The high was mild, nothing like the pure oblivion he got from dust.

"Do you have any dust?"

"No, I stay away from the hard stuff. It will kill you."

Coughing as a cloud of smoke flew from his lips, Jordan shot back "And this won't?"

"Not if used in moderation. So all these people after you, what are you going to do about that?"

"Show them love, right?" Jordan responded, laughing.

William nodded. "Sure, but sounds like you have some serious threats."

"I don't know, William, I don't know. Maybe I should have stayed with Rob and fled to Copenhagen."

"Well, that's an idea. Let it sit for now, get some sleep. I'll go get the guest room ready for you."

The next morning Jordan awoke with the sunrise at five

o'clock. He made his way to the coffee shop and was greeted by Hannah with a warm "Good morning!"

Ten seconds after he entered the shop, he heard the haunting voice of C.L. entering the store "The fuck you think you're doing, boy?"

Panicked, Jordan darted for the entryway, but C.L. grabbed him and tackled him to the ground. "You can't run from me, you little fucker."

"The DEA drained you man, what difference does my few grand make? You're fucked!"

"You helping the DEA? I'm going to have fun killing you, kid. Now get in the fucking van."

C.L. grabbed Jordan by the arm and began dragging him out of the store toward the red van parked out in front of the shop.

"Let him go!" Ali shouted, walking around the side of the building from the parking lot.

"Fuck off old man. I ought to slit your throat while I'm at it."

"Let him go or I will shoot you!" Ali responded, revealing a gun in his right hand.

"Put that away, you don't know hot to use it." C.L. responded, opening the back door of the van and tossing Jordan inside, slamming the door shut as soon as Jordan hit the floor of the van.

Jordan heard a "pop" sound followed by three more successive "pops" and a loud thud against the side of the van. No one else was inside, the front seats were empty and the keys were in the ignition. Crawling up to the drivers seat, Jordan started the van and saw Ali standing in front of the coffee shop, gun in hand, staring at the van in shock, not moving a limb. The gun fell from Ali's hand and he followed it close behind, collapsing on to his knees and looking down at the pavement. C.L. was out of sight, but it was clear to Jordan that he must be laying dead outside of the van. Pausing, Jordan hesitated, unsure whether to drive off or stay. After what felt like an hour, he finally switched off the ignition. Jordan exited from the driver's side door, concerned that his fingerprints were now all over the van and he had no idea how to remove them. He crossed the street and sat beside Ali.

Sirens began ringing out from all directions, Ali's hands were trembling as he looked up and stared into Jordan's eyes. Sweat was beading on his forehead, sitting wordless watching as the police cars blocked off the street, closely followed by several ambulances.

"Run!" Ali whispered, nodding down toward the waterfront.

Jordan looked down the street, then back to Ali, finally turning back to look into the store, where Hannah was standing outside of the entryway, motionless and pale as a ghost. He shook his head, looking back at Ali and responded "No, you just saved my life."

"They will lock us both up if you stay, go Jordan, you must!"

"No, you didn't do anything wrong and I will make sure they know that. If anyone deserves to be locked up, it's me."

Three uniformed police officers walked up to Jordan and Ali, one reaching down with a gloved hand and taking the pistol from the pavement.

"What happened here?" one of them asked.

Ali tried to respond but his voice failed him and tears emerged from his eyes, he stared helplessly at the officers and then looked to Jordan for words.

"He saved me. That man grabbed me out of the store and was going to kill me. Ali shot him."

The officers all turned their gaze to Ali, he looked up at them and nodded his head.

"We need to take you down to the station for some more questions. Is this your gun?"

The officers were looking at Jordan, but he shook his head and pointed to Ali.

"Mine." Ali was barely able to utter in response.

A fourth officer was talking with Hannah, Jordan looked around and saw several additional officers surrounding the van and taking photos. He thought about how stupid it was for him to even have considered driving away, now his fingerprints were on the steering wheel, he wasn't sure what to say when they asked about that. C.L.'s body was covered and being transferred to a long wooden board.

Jordan stood up and offered his hand to help Ali up. Once the two were standing they followed the officers to one of the police cars and were led into the backseat. After getting away with so many things, Jordan thought it was a bit ironic that it was this series of events that finally led him into police custody.

At the police station they were given water and escorted into a room with a table, four chairs and a large glass mirror along the wall. They were never handcuffed and Jordan thought to himself that must be a good sign. As the officer left them in the room and shut the door behind her, the door clicked shut and a bolt could be heard securing the room from the outside. Several minutes passed by, there was no clock in the room and the police had taken both men's phones when they arrived at the station.

Several more minutes passed by without a sound, Ali and Jordan remained wordless staring at themselves in the giant mirrored glass. Finally, Ali broke the silence.

"What will happen?" he asked Jordan.

"I don't know, they are probably investigating us and waiting to hear what we say in here while we're waiting."

Ali turned his gaze back to the mirror, a worried expression covering his face, lips tense and eyes solemn.

Jordan continued after a brief pause, "We're going to be fine, you're a hero Ali, not a criminal."

"You don't understand, Jordan. My skin, my name, my face, it doesn't matter what I do, I'm always a suspect in this country, never a hero."

Jordan frowned, knowing Ali was speaking the truth and unsure of how to respond. An overwhelming sense of guilt invaded his mind, knowing that he got himself into trouble with C.L. and now he had dragged Ali into his mess for the second time. If he had paid C.L. what he owed he probably never would have gotten into any trouble. If he had never entered into debt with C.L., he could have avoided the present predicament as well. Now C.L. was dead, which was good for him, but while he was in the clear legally he knew he was in the wrong morally.

What was justice? Was it possible for a true system of justice to exist? Justice would have been paying off his debt. Did C.L. deserve to die? After all, he was just operating under a different system of justice than the government. In one court C.L. would have been punished for kidnapping Jordan, but C.L. was attempting to enforce the drug ring's justice when he was shot. In the government's court, C.L. and Jordan should be locked up, but they only knew about C.L.'s offenses. In any case, Ali deserved to be free, and Jordan owed him his life.

CHAPTER TWENTY

THE LATCH ON THE DOOR to the interrogation room clicked and the door swung open as a detective entered, clothed in a suit and tie. She had shoulder-length brown hair and horn-rimmed glasses, a petite figure, her pale white skin and deep green eyes combined with her eastern european facial structure created an intimidating aura. She sat down facing the two men and had two folders and two note pads in her hands that she set on the table in front of her. Looking at Ali, then turning her gaze to Jordan, she placed a notepad and pen in front of each of them then said "I need your stories, don't skip anything."

Ali picked up his pen to begin writing, but paused and seemed to struggle with where to begin. Jordan began writing immediately, then scratched out the first sentence he wrote. Continuing on, he paused half-way through the first page and looked to see if he could make out any of what Ali was writing, but Ali's notepad remained blank.

Jordan re-read what he had written so far, the first sentence, now crossed out, read "C.L. was going to kill me." The second sentence, written after reconsidering how to be honest and seek justice, read "I owed C.L. $13,000 for dust he sold me on credit and I was over three months behind on paying him back." Pausing, Jordan chuckled considering how similar his situation was to those who racked up credit card debt on extraneous clothing and entertainment expenses. Had his debt been with one of those creditors, he never would have had to fear for his life. His notepad went on to describe how C.L. had threatened him, forced him out of his job, and was attempting to kill him so he could collect on a fraudulent life insurance policy. As he continued writing, he detailed how Ali had given him his job back, despite C.L.'s threat and finally saved his life by shooting C.L. His goal was to ensure Ali's freedom, but he also sought his own justice, unsure of exactly what that meant.

Once he was finished writing, Jordan looked over at Ali's paper again and saw just three lines written. Ali's pen laid atop the notepad indicating he was finished writing. Jordan laid his pen down on top of his own notepad and pushed it back toward the detective.

Without a word, the detective took both notepads and began to read them, starting with Ali's. Glancing up at Ali and asking "Nothing else?"

"No, it is simple, ma'am. That man took my employee by force and threatened to kill him, I told him to stop and warned him I would shoot, but he continued and so I shot him to save Jordan."

The detective dropped her gaze back to the notepads and began to read Jordan's account of events. When she finished, she took the pads and folders she had entered with, then exited the room saying "I'll be back."

Two hours passed by, Ali and Jordan remained in the interrogation room wondering whether they were to be free or imprisoned. Jordan's guilt continued to grow on his mind and he convinced himself that he deserved to be imprisoned. It was the only way he could pay for the injustice he had created by not paying C.L. Ali slumped in his chair and looked utterly defeated, as if he were destined for punishment no matter how justified his actions were. Neither uttered a word, their gaze jumping to the door whenever a footstep was heard passing by.

Finally, the detective returned and began talking to them without sitting down.

"We are holding both of you for a few nights while we wait for some test results to come back from the lab." Two officers entered the room as the detective continued, "Officers Brown and Jenkins will take you to holding."

The next day, Jordan awoke to a silent cell, the others sharing the space were still fast asleep. A lack of windows or clocks prevented him from knowing what time it was. He wondered what Rob was doing in Copenhagen, what would have happened if he had gone along with him? Surely he wouldn't be in jail, and neither would Ali. C.L. would probably still be alive, for that matter. Would Pat have still killed himself? It was all in the past, going back over it was a waste of time, yet his mind was running wild with the possibilities. He thought back to his conversations with Hannah and William, they understood his pain but somehow were able to happily live their lives despite the vast injustices surrounding them. They fought evil and corruption with art and education. Yet at the same time they seemed to be okay with the present state of things and the slow progress toward a better future. Jordan wondered if it was a battle worth fighting, or a lost cause? He was all or nothing, unable to comprehend a middle ground. Were William and Hannah just hypocrites for having differing values from their government and choosing to remain a part of it, or was he the one with faulty logic for preferring not to take part at all in a system he opposed?

Jordan went back to the toilet and dropped his pants, hoping that perhaps the fact that all those surrounding him were asleep would allow him to finally relieve himself, having never been in such an exposed situation before. After a few minutes his bowels loosened and he took the shit he had attempted and failed to take before going to sleep the night before.

A while later, others began to wake and police began walking past the holding cell as they began their workday. When Ali awoke, Jordan went to him and asked how he was doing. Ali just shook his head with a sense of utter defeat and misery.

When an officer stopped in front of the cell and called out for Ali and Jordan, the two jumped from their seats on the floor and approached the door.

"You've got a visitor." the officer announced, allowing the two to exit the cell and indicating for them to follow her. As they entered the visiting area they both began to smile when they saw Hannah sitting at an empty table. "Only ten minutes." the officer said as she pointed toward Hannah and walked away.

As they approached the table, Jordan noticed Hannah's cheeks were pink and tears were running down her face, his happiness grew into concern. Hannah had always been a bastion of light and perseverance to him, if she was concerned than things must not be going well.

"What's going on?" he asked as he sat down with Ali across from her.

"I've been worried sick about you two, it's just not fair that you're locked up here. Have you heard about Pat?"

"No..."

"They are saying he was responsible for the Internet and power outages, they're calling him a deranged psychopath."

Jordan sighed with relief, then saw Hannah glare at him and he looked down at the ground, unsure what to think. He had been convinced that everything would be pinned on him, one way or another the police would charge him not only for C.L.'s murder, but also the outages, he had lost all hope and this news was a glimmer of the miraculous. Yet with his unexpected relief came more guilt, after all it was his idea to create the outages and C.L. had been after him for good reason. As his luck increased so did his guilt and it was beginning to feel unbearable.

"Pat wasn't a psycho, he may have been ill but he had a good heart. I still don't understand how he lost hope."

"He had no love in his life, Jordan. Isn't it obvious? We need love just as much as air and water. He had been deprived of love, devoting his life to his work and getting only money in return."

"How is the shop?" Interrupted Ali, staring up at the clock knowing every minute was precious.

"I've been working open to close, business is back to normal but everyone keeps asking about you. What should I tell them?"

"Only the truth, Hannah."

"But when will you get out?"

"They're running some tests apparently, I don't know how long that takes."

"But you already admitted to shooting him, what sort of test would they need to run?"

Ali shrugged, looking down at the table. He knew there was more going on than the police would tell him, they were probably running watchlist and background checks.

"Find ways to make the time pass, guys. You will go nuts in there otherwise. Focus on your art Jordan, no more schemes!"

Jordan nodded, he hadn't given a moments thought to art. Staring at the iron bars of the holding cell captivated him, he was drenched in fear that consumed every ounce of his attention.

Hannah slid a pad of blank drawing paper and a piece of charcoal to Jordan and simply said "Draw."

Their visiting time had passed by quickly and the officer approached to lead Jordan and Ali back into holding.

"God bless you, Hannah." Ali said as the two walked away.

Back in the holding cell, Jordan sat on the concrete floor with his back leaning against the iron bars. He laid the pad of paper Hannah had given him on his crossed legs and held the piece of charcoal in his hand. He was not sure where to start. He had never taken an art class. He knew nothing about charcoal. He thought back to the drawings he made at Ann's house after having that crazy dream, the images resonated in his mind and demanded being preserved on paper, he had no choice at that time. But what was demanding to be drawn now? Looking around, he decided to start with what he saw in front of him, the cell bars and the police walking back and forth. As he drew a narrow, dark line down the left side of the paper, he wished he had more colors than black, he didn't want to make things any more depressing than they already were.

Having finished drawing the cell wall, he attempted to draw a stick figure walking past, but the legs and arms looked as if they were part of the iron bars of the cell wall, there was no way to tell the depth of the scene. Unable to erase anything, he continued drawing lines between the cell bars, creating some sort of abstract geometric drawing. Soon the cell bars were no longer cell bars, but equal parts of the imaginative art. The lines he was drawing between the bars began to curve and form new patterns. In the center, he created a rough outline of a flower.

Jordan sat the charcoal down on the ground beside him and stared at what he had created. *What-he-had-created.* The fears that had terrorized him earlier were entirely gone, replaced with an overwhelming sense of empowerment. He recalled the similar way he felt after drawing out his dreams, all of the things that worried him lost their power when compared with the beauty of his creation. Gazing at his work he was impressed, he didn't know he was capable of creating art, it had turned out better than he thought was possible.

He got up to show Ali what he had created, finding him sitting in the corner, eyes closed in silent meditation, as he had been doing since they were first put into holding. Not wanting to interrupt him, Jordan sat directly in front of him and mimicked his form to attempt his own meditation. As his eyes closed he saw the image of Hannah in his mind, her smiling face and bright eyes illuminated the darkness of his psyche. The thought of showing her what he created passed through his mind, then the thought of giving it to her. Yes he decided, that is what he would do, as soon as they were let out he would give her his drawing.

Suddenly Ali's voice interrupted his thoughts "I didn't know you practiced meditation, Jordan."

"I don't meditate, I'm just copying you."

"You may do more meditation than you think you do."

"Look at what I made!" Jordan shouted with youthful enthusiasm, holding up his drawing in front of Ali.

"You're an artist too? So much I never knew about you, Jordan!"

"It's the second thing I've ever drawn."

"Brilliant, it's beautiful!"

A voice from one of the guards interrupted their discussion, "Ali, Jordan, the detective is ready for you."

They entered the familiar interrogation room and sat down, only a few minutes passed before the detective joined them.

"You're free to go, gentlemen. You have Hannah and the CCTV at the bank across the street to thank. We may need you over the next few weeks, so stay in town."

A deep sigh of relief came from Ali, a smile from ear to ear burst onto Jordan's face. The two looked at each other in disbelief and joy.

CHAPTER TWENTY-ONE

H ANNAH WAS WAITING FOR ALI and Jordan outside of the police station, she carried a knowing smile, as if their freedom had never been in question. Her car, a 1996 Honda Civic, sat idling behind her. Jordan looked around, the sun shining brightly amidst a clear blue sky. Turning his gaze to Ali, he saw a wave of relaxation and relief wash over the man's face.

"Get in, let's blow this joint!" Hannah shouted as the two slowly walked toward her. Ali and Jordan began running toward her, just as eager as she was to get away from the police station.

As they got into the car, Jordan joining Hannah in the front upon Ali's insistence, a black SUV started its engine across the parking lot from them. Hannah slammed on the gas and sped out of the station toward downtown. Ali looked back and saw the black SUV following them, turn for turn, always right behind them. He sighed, realizing that things were not entirely back to normal.

As they traversed the streets of Seattle, Jordan stared out his window taking in everything that went by. Building cranes stood scattered throughout the city, newly opened buildings with their "for lease" signs displayed in empty retail suites. People walked down the sidewalk while staring at their smartphones, barely managing not to run into each other. All the men wearing either traditional suits or the new tech suit: a plaid shirt and jeans. Traffic grew dense as they approached the city center and Jordan couldn't help but count the vast majority of cars that each held only a single individual sitting in the driver's seat. Nothing had changed, but at the same time these things didn't bother him as much now. Unwinding history was not as easy as he had hoped, he learned that the hard way. The small amount of damage he and Pat had inflicted had healed within days, a minor disruption, a news story, nothing more. No revolution, no change in social conscious.

Jordan grew sad as his thoughts turned to Pat, how had there not been more signs the man was suicidal? He could have done something, he could have been there for him. Jordan knew what it was like to feel hopeless, he might have been able to make up for all the times others had motivated him to hang on. Instead Pat was gone, there was nothing that could be done.

"Cheer up, Jordan. You're a free man! The world is your oyster, and it needs you. It needs your art." Hannah said, watching as Jordan slouched down in his seat.

Hannah's words reminded Jordan about the drawing he made in the holding cell for her. A smile broke out across his face. But as he looked back out at the people walking by, he couldn't see how his art made any real difference in the world. What did those passersby care about his art? About any art? They were creatures subservient to the kingdom of things, the only reason they cared about art was if it was worth a lot of money. What made one person's art worth more than another's anyway? How does someone who doesn't appreciate art value it so highly? The depression slipped back into his mind and he tore his gaze away from the outside world to Hannah. She was smiling. How did she look out upon this sick, dark world and smile?

"What does anyone care for art? How does art change anything?" He asked.

"Always the pessimist, aren't you? When people walk into our store do you think their experience is heightened by the art? By the flowers? Do you think maybe they come back because of the art? Maybe they will never admit it, Jordan, but art always has an impact. People want to see it, perhaps even desperately. They may not be so keen to admit it, but its still the truth. Art reminds us we're human."

Jordan took a deep breath, inhaling until his lungs were full and holding the air within him. She was right, he knew it. But how could she not be overwhelmed by the darkness? How did she not see it?

Exhaling, he responded, "I drew something while we were waiting to be released."

"Oh did you? Show me, Jordan! Show me!"

"I will, when we get to the shop."

"They're following us." Ali interjected.

"Who?"

"That black truck behind us. It's been following us since we left the police station."

Jordan looked back, noticing the SUV for the first time. "It must be C.L.'s crew. Shit. Fuck. I am always screwing things up. They're after me, not you guys. Just let me out."

"I saw them too, probably just police curious where we're going." Hannah responded.

"Stay in the car, Jordan. No reason to get in a panic." Ali ordered.

"No, I couldn't live with them bringing either of you to any harm. You've already saved my life and I can't risk you getting in any more danger." Jordan unfastened his seat belt. "Pull over, Hannah. Please."

Hannah came to a stop at a red light. Jordan opened his door and leapt from the car before anyone could stop him. Slamming the passenger door shut behind him, he began running perpendicular to the car, down the cross street. Hannah's car came around the corner, back window rolled down and Ali looking at him desperately, "You're just drawing suspicion Jordan, get back in the car!"

The black SUV continued to follow them, blatantly interested in what was going on, but silent with the windows rolled up and tinted so that all Jordan could see through the windshield was two men in suits.

"No, just go. I'll be fine. Let me deal with my problem, please!"

He began walking toward the SUV, approaching the passenger window he shouted "What do you want? Your business is gone, why do I matter so much to you?"

The man sitting in the passenger seat didn't respond, the window remained rolled up. Jordan stepped out in front of the SUV. Continuing to shout, "I'm sick of being on the run! If you want me, come and get me. I'm right here."

The truck turned and zoomed around Jordan, pulling alongside Hannah's car.

"Get back in, Jordan!" Ali shouted.

"No, this ends now." Jordan tried to open the back door of the truck. Finding it was locked, he approached the passenger door but failed to open it as well. He pounded on the passenger window, shouting "Talk to me!" with no response from the men within the truck.

A police car pulled up behind the SUV, its lights flashing and siren chirping on and off. The loudspeaker on the front of the car amplified the voice of the police officer "Step away from the vehicle, sir."

Jordan looked over at the police car, taking a step back from the SUV. At that moment the SUV zoomed off down the street. A second passed by, the officer in the car looking puzzled and unsure what to do. Finally the police chose to pursue the SUV, shouting "Pull to the side of the road" out of its speaker.

Jordan watched the chase, then got back into Hannah's car sitting idle on the side of the road.

"I told you it was C.L.'s crew."

"You don't know that, Jordan." Ali responded.

Hannah entered traffic, following the police car and the SUV. The SUV was not pulling over and the police car's siren was on full blast now. The SUV continued up Union street and turned down 5th avenue. Another police car was waiting for it, blocking the entire lane. Trapped, the SUV stopped and the two men stepped out from the front seats.

Hannah pulled over behind one of the police cars that were now surrounding the SUV. Jordan got back out of the car and walked toward the SUV. An officer grabbed him by the shoulder and told him to stay back. He paused, standing next to the officer without a word.

"Step out, on your knees, hands on your head." an officer shouted, gun drawn, walking toward the two men in the truck. Each of them followed the officer's instructions.

The incident had turned into a scene, traffic stopped, police cars all over the place, passersby gawking and taking photos with their smartphones. A disruption, an incident, news. Tomorrow this would be nothing but old news. Today it was on Twatwire, trending on Facefeed. While dozens of people snapped photos and tapped in hashtags, hundreds of others walking down sidewalks in other parts of the city stared at their phones in eager interest to follow the emerging drama. It was instant, it was now, it was shared. No one truly cared, they just wanted to be entertained. Jordan continued to observe.

As the two men from the SUV sat on their knees with hands on their heads a handful of police officers surrounded them. A few seconds passed, there was a conversation occurring that Jordan couldn't hear. One of the men put his hands down from his head and reached in his jacket to pull out a wallet, handing it to one of the officers. The other man followed closely after, doing the same thing. Both of them returned their hands to their heads.

"These don't look like drug dealers to me, Jordan. I'm no expert, but I think Ali was right. They are just following us from the police station to see what we do."

"Maybe, but you don't know what the higher-ups look

like. How do you know someone is a criminal just based on the clothes they wear? The car they drive?"

"I'm just saying." Hannah responded, a bit wounded. She returned to her car, losing interest in the matter. Ali was still in the back seat, looking out his window on the scene.

One of the officers approached Jordan with an urgent step. "Those are FBI agents you were harassing, you know? You're lucky they don't want to press charges against you."

Jordan admitted to himself at this moment that indeed he was being paranoid. The whole C.L. saga was in the past, it was over and done with. Why was he still looking over his shoulder all the time?

"They were following us for miles, but I'm lucky you didn't arrest me?"

"They didn't do anything illegal, you did."

Jordan sighed, lips sealed tight, holding his tongue. He had no interest in getting on the wrong side of the law, after all he was lucky to be a free man after everything he had already done. He looked up at the officer, and with as much authenticity as he could muster, said "Thank you."

The two men in suits got back into their SUV, the police cars slowly scattered back throughout the city from the scene of the incident. Jordan stared at the SUV as the doors closed and the engine started. He walked back to Hannah's car and silently returned to the passenger seat, closing the door and fastening his seat belt. He broke the silence by simply stating "You were right."

As they drove back toward the coffee shop, Jordan couldn't help but look over his shoulder. The SUV had resumed following them. He turned his gaze to Ali, sitting behind him, and saw that Ali too had noticed and was watching the SUV trailing them.

"So we just let the FBI follow us wherever we go? This is normal, legal and not a violation of our privacy or rights?"

"Welcome to America, land of the free."

As they continued the remaining two miles to the coffee shop, Jordan tried to ignore the SUV and resume observing the people they passed by on the street. He noticed that not everyone was a mindless drone, some people were wearing regular clothes, clothes that were more than six months old, some people waited at bus stops, there were women walking their young children down the sidewalk. Asian, white, black, hispanic, there was diversity in the city, at least on this street. Where were they all going? What did they do? They certainly were not regular guests in the coffee shop. Maybe they didn't have $5 to spare on a cup of steamed milk.

Arriving at the coffee shop, Jordan saw it was staffed by two people he didn't recognize. There was a small queue at the register and two couples sitting at tables.

"Ok, show me!" Hannah said directly to Jordan.

He was eager to show her what he had drawn. As he sorted through his bag to find it he remembered how he had felt when he was drawing it, unsure whether he would ever be let out, unsure what he might be accused of.

"Jordan Santarelli?" a voice came from the store entrance.

Turning around, Jordan saw the two men in suits who had been driving the SUV. They were older than he originally thought they were, now that he could see them up close he could see the wrinkles in their skin, greying hair tucked beneath their caps, and one of them was walking with a cane. As he examined the cane, its long black metallic shaft and rounded polished steel head, a shiver of fear ran through his spine. He recognized the cane, the cane used to beat him in the back of the car C.L.'s boss had picked him up in. Was this the same man? Staring into the dark, swollen eyes of the man carrying the cane he could see nothing but hatred. It was impossible to tell if this was the same man Jordan remembered, it had been so dark in the car he never clearly made out the man's face. But he recognized the cane, with its shining steel head.

"What do you want? Why were you following us?" He asked in anger.

"It's time to repay your debt, Jordan." Said the man with the cane.

The other man grabbed Jordan by the arm and led him out of the store. Jordan dropped his bag with the drawing on the ground. He couldn't believe this was happening. Why did they care so much about his $10,000 debt? Weren't they bankrupt? This was ridiculous. And how did they pass for FBI agents earlier? His paranoia was on overload, he had been right all along. This was ridiculous. He let the man lead him out, with C.L.'s boss following behind them. Turning his head back he shouted "Not this time, Ali. Not this time."

CHAPTER TWENTY-TWO

JORDAN'S MIND WAS ON FIRE. Was this finally the end? A failed existence. He had finally made an attempt to stand up and change things for the better, only to fail miserably. Years of idle addiction, no family, and now this? He needed more time. Only thirty years old, a third of the way through a normal lifespan. There had to be something he could do.

As he was tossed into the backseat of the SUV, he quickly righted himself and watched as the door slammed shut beside him. The driver pulled away while Jordan's assailant looked back at him and said "We need to talk."

As the truck entered the interstate, the man continued, "My name is Garber, Bill Garber. You're right, the organization went tits up after the DEA's sting operation. The best I could do is make out with a stash and save my own life. I have no interest in you or your debt."

"So why am I here?" Jordan asked, still carrying a deep sense of foreboding and trying to come up with an escape plan.

"Your employer killed my employee who was just doing his job attempting to collect your debt. Now you owe me your life." Bill paused, mentally debating whether to continue.

"If you know about the sting operation, Jordan, then you might have more information that could prove valuable to me." Bill said as he nearly choked on the phlegm that inflected on each word that came from his mouth.

His sagging jawline, worn skin and gravel-ridden voice gave Jordan a new impression of the man he had previously been so afraid of. Bill was just another human, an old one at that. He was strong, but in poor health and recently suffered the loss of his entire enterprise. The only leverage he had over Jordan was this speeding truck and the untold, unseen weapons in the front.

Jordan remained silent in the back seat, turning his gaze from Bill to the city passing by. You couldn't see people from the highway, only buildings. How many people were in all those buildings? What were they doing?

After several minutes passed by, Bill continued, "You have one way to get out of this situation alive. We are driving south to a private dock, when we get there I will bind your feet, anchor you and let you sink to the bottom. Before you die, you'll see the remains of the others who have suffered the same fate. Then you'll try to escape, panic, gasp for air, inhale water, and choke to death. Or, if you are cooperative, I could make things go a bit more smoothly for you."

How could such an old, suffering man be so dark? How many people had he actually killed? Was he all talk, or was he really as evil as his words made him out to be? Some old men had grandkids, this one had skeletons in his closet, quite literally. What made a man go this way instead of another, happier way?

"Why do you do what you do, Bill? Why not give it

up? Stop being a ruthless asshole drug lord and find a nice woman to settle down with? Who took your heart, Bill?"

Now it was Bill's turn to be silent. The man's face was stone cold and motionless, his lips shut tight, not allowing any sign of emotion to slip out. His eyes gazed out ahead at the open highway. Minutes past by and Jordan felt a spark of victory, the man's silence alone indicated that he had been struck. Jordan grinned and saw Bill look up at the rear view mirror to catch his smile.

"I do it for the money, kid. It's a family business I inherited from my pa and he carried on from my grandpa. There was never a choice, it wasn't something I decided to do. I do what I do because it's my job, it's the right thing to do."

"The right thing to do?" Jordan laughed. "You fucked up Bill, the business is bankrupt! And no choice? That's bullshit, you always have a choice. You just don't want to admit that you have done everything you've done willingly."

"Enough! You're wasting the final moments of your life, Jordan. Now tell me what you know, tell me how you found out about the sting. You can save yourself by proving yourself useful, or you can die keeping your secrets."

Jordan evaluated his situation, he had to have more options than Bill laid out. He had no phone, but Ali and Hannah knew he had been taken. Maybe they called the police? He could jump out of the truck, but leaping from a vehicle going 70 miles per hour down a busy highway had as much of a risk of death as staying with Bill. He looked up at Bill and the man driving the car, who had remained silent since Jordan was captured. Could he take the two of them? How strong were they? Strong enough to drag him from the store into the car, but they were old, Jordan had to have some sort of advantage over them if he put some effort into it.

Could he send a distress signal from the car? He had no paper, no pen. He stared down at the t-shirt he was wearing, wondering if he could signal someone with it. None of these options seemed very viable to him, but he was confident that there was a way out he had not thought of yet.

"Suit yourself." Bill responded to Jordan's silence. They continued driving south down the highway for another half hour, finally taking an exit in what appeared to be the middle of nowhere. The truck winded through a wooded road, no cars were in front of them or behind them. No cars passed by in the opposite direction either. The evergreen trees towered far above the road, the sun shining through their branches and illuminating the shrubs below. As they continued, the road turned to a series of switchbacks as it descended down. Jordan assumed the water had to be approaching. He tried to imagine making his escape, this road was long and the hill was steep. Running through the forest away from the road was his only chance of success, forcing Bill to pursue him on foot rather than with his truck. Even if he managed to escape, where was he? Where was civilization from here? How did he get home?

The car turned down a dirt road and Jordan could see a small cabin perched down at the end. As the truck approached the cabin he saw five young men in black suits emerge from the cabin and standby waiting for their arrival. So much for making a break for it.

"Meet the men who will take your life, Jordan. I'm too old to do the work myself, you see. But I still enjoy watching."

One of the young men opened Jordan's door and dragged him out, tossing him to the ground without a word and knocking the wind from his lungs. Jordan gasped for air. When he finally caught his breath, he tried to look up at the man, but a boot heel quickly pressed against the side of his face, pinning his head to the ground.

At the same time, another man grabbed Jordan's hands and bound them behind his back. Jordan began to sweat, his looming death was suddenly feeling much more real than it had while riding in the backseat down the highway while Bill described how he would be killed.

No police had come to the rescue, there wasn't a trace of help on the way. Jordan began to realize how grim his situation was and felt tears join the sweat on his face. This wasn't fair, this wasn't right. What was his move here? He could see no escape, no hope, certain death minutes away.

After binding his feet together, three of the men carried Jordan's body around the side of the cabin and on to a dock that stretched a quarter of the way into a small lake. They dropped him on the dock and he suddenly felt his humanity slipping away from his soul. He was now nothing more than meat, an animal being sent to pasture. The other two young men at the cabin carried a large concrete block onto the dock, it had rebar arched across the top with each end buried into the block. As the men laid the block sideways next to his feet, the other three distributed themselves between holding Jordan in place and tying his feet through the rebar loop on the concrete block.

Jordan thought he would have more time to talk his way out of this, opportunities for escape, this was happening too fast. How much time did he have left?

Looking up at Bill, who was standing on the dock watching everything happen, expressionless, motionless, Jordan saw pure emptiness in the man's eyes. Had he ever had a soul? When did he let it go? Was this man truly evil, was there a shred of good in him? How many times had he watched this happen before? Bill was not a man, he was a machine, operating according to a pre-programmed script, no love in his life, no hope, just carrying out his role in the grand machine of society. How could Jordan break through and bring Bill back to life? He certainly could not do anything if he was dead.

"The DEA agent!" Jordan screamed in desperation, catching his breath before continuing, "I know about the undercover DEA agent that worked for you." He looked up, unsure whether speaking would do him any good at this point.

"Is that all you've got?" Bill asked, with a grimace on his face.

The unnamed men continued to bind Jordan to the concrete block, not even pausing at the exchange between him and Bill. When he finished tying Jordan to the block, two of the men lifted up the block while another two lifted his torso and held him over the water.

Jordan was ready to tell Bill everything, he was willing to do anything to save his life and knew that speaking was his only hope. Yet the immense fear that was pulsing through his veins made it impossible for words to come out no matter how hard he tried. Gasping for air, moving his lips, he was unable to make a sound. He closed his eyes and clenched his jaw, took a deep breath and with every ounce of energy he could muster exclaimed "She's married to the CEO of Facefeed."

"Put him back on the dock. I want to hear more." Bill ordered.

The men did as instructed, laying Jordan back down on the dock, still bound to the block.

Jordan felt a rush of hope surge through him, he thought of Hannah, Ali and William, all of the people who had given him a glimmer of hope and inspiration. What would they do in this situation? He took a deep breath, never before realizing how precious each living moment was in his life. Looking up at Bill, he began to tell him everything he knew. The sun was setting as Jordan continued reciting his account of the events that had ensued since his initial encounter with Bill. Desperate to demonstrate his value, he spewed details of the Internet and power schemes, Pat's suicide and Rob's fleeing to Denmark. Finally catching up to the present, he stopped and looked up at Bill like a puppy desperate for its owners affection.

Bill looked out over the lake, he appeared to be thinking, his eyes formed a contemplative expression. Jordan closed his eyes and said a prayer, the first time he had ever attempted to converse with the divine, he wasn't even sure who he was praying to. Opening his eyes, Jordan turned his gaze out to the sun setting over the lake. It was beautiful, igniting the sky with orange, red and yellow hues traced through the scattered clouds. The lake was still and reflected the surrounding trees and magnificent sunset.

"Leave him here, we'll decide his fate in the morning." Bill said to the men as he quickly turned around and walked back toward the cabin without even glancing at Jordan.

CHAPTER
TWENTY-THREE

JORDAN WATCHED BILL WALK AWAY, followed by the men who had tied him up. They left him laying on the dock, hands and feet still bound, anchored to the giant concrete block. He had no choice but to continue laying on his back, lacking the strength to pull himself up to a seated position. He took a deep breath and stared up at the sky, feeling an unexpected sense of peace about whatever was to come next, grateful for the fact that he was still alive.

He never heard the engine of the SUV start up, so he reasoned that Bill and the men must be staying inside the cabin. Jordan wasn't tired, his eyes wide open and heart still racing from his near-death experience. He let the current of his mind flow without giving any of the thoughts, mostly fears and worries, any of the attention they were used to receiving from him.

The sky grew darker and stars began to emerge, first just a handful, but soon it seemed as if the entire sky was illuminated by hundreds of tiny white specks. When was the last time he had seen the stars? Living indoors, always hustling around, it was easy to forget they even existed. He often forgot we were flying around in a solar system the size of which our human minds could barely comprehend. So much space, an enormous, endlessly expansive universe. They were all just dust flying in the void. What really mattered? Debts to drug dealers, whether or not we had electricity, people selling their souls for a chance at the American dream? It was all so small in the big picture. Why should it even matter to him? This brief mortality, this miracle of life on the big blue marble, what was he to do with it? His thoughts returned to Hannah, Ali and William. He remembered the framed photographs of William with his wife and kids on the living room table. Love. That was what he was here for, to help spread love and happiness. Nothing else mattered.

Time passed by. Stars moved ever so slowly across the sky., but they actually weren't moving at all, Jordan was the one moving. No, Jordan was laying still on the dock. Earth, the Earth was moving in its glorious daily revolution as it slowly made its annual journey around the Sun. The Sun, center of our solar system, led all the planets traveling through the galaxy to an unknown destination. What an amazing spaceship, to live here, right now, in this moment, it was glorious.

The stars disappeared from Jordan's view as his eyes shut and sleep slowly flowed into him. His chest rising with each inhale of breath, his heart gently beating life through his body.

Looking around, Jordan saw the lake had turned deep purple. He was now standing on his feet, no longer bound. Turning to his left he saw the giant block he had been tied to, but it now had feet of its own and the rebar loop on top had become a large eyeball. A deep gash in the front of the block formed what appeared to be a smile. Jordan looked at the block, staring into its enormous, singular eyeball. The eyeball stared back at him.

"Cyclops, do you speak?" he asked.

The gash that formed a smile grew broader, but no words were uttered. Instead the block's feet began to move and jump up and down, emitting a myriad of clicking and clacking. It was a smiling, tap dancing, cyclops concrete block. Jordan stared in awe, a smile growing on his own face. As the little jig came to an end, the block looked back at Jordan, its grin turning into a flat lip and its eye staring at him in anticipation.

"Me?"

The block nodded by bowing ever so slightly forward.

"I can't dance."

The block walked toward Jordan, a determined look on its face, speeding up as it approached him. Jordan feared it might knock him into the glowing water, unsure what to do, he leaped over the block and turned around. The block made an about-face as well, a small grin returning to its face and a slight nod of approval, but also tilting itself sideways jeering for more.

Jordan was not interested in dancing with a concrete block on the dock. He gazed at the glowing purple lake surrounding him, it was opaque and he couldn't help but wonder what that strange liquid felt like and what might be hidden within its depths. Was it warm or cold? Why did it glow? Could he drink it? Would it feel like water, or a prickly fur? Looking back at the block and seeing its grin turn into a glare, he decided enough was enough and leaped, executing a perfect backflip as he dove into the lake.

Bounding through the air, head and torso tucked in as his body rotated toward the lake, he thought to himself how good it felt to be free of gravity, even just for a moment. To be up in the air, flying as it were, looking down at the helpless block and descending toward the unknown mystery within the glowing purple lake.

Gravity soon resumed control and he began to descend head-first into the lake, breaking its mirror-like stillness and entering the unknown. It was warm, Jordan felt flush, as if he had just walked in to a living room with a roaring fireplace, leaving behind a bitter winter storm. He stretched his arms out to take it all in, the warmth flowed through him, igniting his muscles, veins and heart. Without thinking, he breathed in the water and felt the warmth envelop his mouth and throat as it flowed into his lungs. He didn't choke or gag or gasp for breath, but to his own surprise the water came into his body as naturally as air and felt like breathing. He exhaled and then took in another breath of the liquid, delighting in how fresh and nourishing it felt.

The glowing purple haze enveloped him and he looked out to try and see what was around him but only saw the bright glowing purple, as if he had left Earth and become part of a color within a vast spectrum of light, nothing else existed. He was suspended in the liquid neon color and as he propelled himself forward with his arms he felt the rush of the warm softness glide along his skin. The bright glow of the purple substance persisted and nothing else entered his perception. He couldn't even see his own arms. As time passed, it became difficult to track whether he had been in the lake for a minute or an hour. He continued propelling himself forward, but no matter where he went it felt and appeared the same as where he had come from. Was he even moving?

Jordan took a deep breath in and turned his head up to swim back to the surface of the lake, convinced he had seen all there was to see in the lake. As he swam up and up he saw nothing but more glowing purple haze. Minutes, hours, days, years, centuries passed by. It was unthinkable that he had not reached the surface by now, his breath began to quicken, but the strange liquid that was flowing in and out of his lungs seemed to bring a great calm to him and he stopped moving, stopped struggling, stopped thinking about how to escape and just sat in the haze, with his eyes wide open, contemplating the nature of reality.

As he floated in silence, drawing in a slow, deep breath, he heard bells playing a quiet melody in the distance. The tune slowly grew in volume and as it grew it seemed to be coming from every direction at once. The melody was mesmerizing and began steering Jordan's thoughts, he went from his deep philosophical contemplation to remembering the shared joy he felt when he looked to Ali as they were informed of their freedom. That shared moment, the wide grins, it was greater than each of them separately. He recalled his experience with William and Hannah trying to talk him down from his madness, their compassion as he struggled with Pat's suicide, their shelter, their friendship.

Suddenly the image of his mother burst into his

mind's eye and he immediately began to weep. Overcome with sadness, ashamed of how he had lived his life, irresponsible, pleasure-seeking, not caring. A wave of guilt crashed into his psyche as he thought of how ignorant he had been of his mother's sacrifices to raise him, the struggles she went through with his father's reckless behavior and abandonment.

Jordan had not spoken with his mother in years, his addiction to dust had made everything else in life unimportant unless it stood in the way of him getting his next fix. The thought of her had not even crossed his mind in months. She lived far away, her career taking her to Europe where she taught at…a school he couldn't remember the name of. He held a deep-seeded resentment for her leaving to the other side of the world just after he finished High School. After suffering his father's escape to Asia, he had felt bitterly alone when she announced her departure. But now his memory refreshed as he recalled her offer for him to join her and live abroad. He had no interest in living away from the town he grew up in and never considered that being close to family may be more important. At the time, he thought her offer wasn't even real, he had told himself that she didn't actually want him to go with her.

As the thoughts flooded through his mind, accompanied by images of his loving mother, Jordan floated in the lake and took in everything. Drums and horns began to play along with the bells, creating an intoxicating melody. Soon strings joined in and the music seemed to flow with the thoughts racing through his mind, creating an overwhelming wave of emotion in his heart. The glow of the lake intensified and began to pulse with the music, everything was in lock-step harmony and Jordan remained still, tears pouring down his cheeks.

Suddenly he recognized what he was feeling, the emotion so long absent from his heart. It was love. True, genuine, pure love. The memory of the selfless sacrifices his mother made for him over so many years unlocked a floodgate of emotion, for the first time he recognized what the word love truly meant. How had he not understood it until now? He had never acted selflessly or sacrificed anything for anyone in his life. He saw the vast difference between his lustful desire for sexual gratification at the sight of every attractive woman who passed by on the street or entered the store and what true love really meant. Finally, he understood how he might fill the growing void in his soul. Love was sacrifice, love was work, love was devotion to another's growth and wellbeing without seeking anything in return. He had been blind for so many years, for all of his life. This moment, this experience in the lake had unlocked his heart, opened his mind. He now saw the purpose of his life, the purpose of art in the broadest sense. It was to love, to sacrifice, to build community.

The lake went dark, then disappeared entirely. At the same moment, Jordan felt his stomach jump into his throat as he descended into nothingness, falling quickly. He looked down in the direction of his fall, but could see only darkness. He shouted but no sound came out. The music was gone and panic had wiped out all the other thoughts in his mind. He waved his arms and legs, reaching out for anything to stop his fall, but he continued to descend. Falling further and further, he looked up and saw the same nothingness that was below him. Attempting another plea for help, he gasped as he realized he not only couldn't speak, but he couldn't breathe. Suffocating, he closed his eyes and prayed, prayed for his mother, prayed for forgiveness, prayed for a chance to live.

Jordan continued to fall and gasp for breath, his lungs throbbing and his mind losing the sense of his limbs. Suddenly he felt his back slam into the hard wooden planks of the dock, a burst of light flooded his vision followed by a shockwave of immense pain throughout his body. He breathed in, his lungs filling with air and his senses slowly returning. He breathed out and breathed in again, deeply, filling his lungs. As he exhaled his second breath he began to smell fire, smoke. His eyes opened and he saw giant clouds of smoke floating above him, all around him. Breathing in the smoke-filled air, his throat began to itch, coated with the soot and grime from each successive breath.

He tried to stand up and see where all the smoke was coming from, but he couldn't move his feet. Looking down he saw that he was still anchored to the giant cement block. Twisting his torso to try and see the cabin, he gazed around and saw that it was intact and without any signs of fire. The source of the smoke was unclear and his surroundings were barely visible as the clouds of smoke grew denser.

The stomp of boots walking down the dock alerted Jordan to the reality he had fallen asleep from. He saw the speechless, young men who had tied him up and nearly drowned him approach. The inspiration from his dream returned to his mind and his fists shook in rage at the restraint holding him immobile, powerless to begin making things right.

The men leaned over him and began to cut through the ropes binding his feet, but they left his hands tied behind his back. Without a word, they lifted him up and carried him back to the shore. He heard the SUV's engine start as one of the men opened the rear door while the two carrying him tossed his body into the back seat. Jordan struggled to sit up, and when he did, he saw Bill and the other older man in the front seats.

As the door shut behind him, the driver turned the truck around and began ascending the hill away from the cabin and the lake, back toward civilization.

CHAPTER
TWENTY-FOUR

S MOKE WAS EVERYWHERE, BUT FIRE was nowhere. Jordan looked out his window as the SUV made its way up the switchbacks and could only see a few yards in any direction before everything turned to dark grey clouds of smoke. There was no sign of a fire or even which direction all the smoke was coming from. Despite the best efforts of the truck's air filter, a growing amount of haze could be seen inside and there was a strong smell of burning timber. Jordan breathed in and choked on the heavily polluted air, his breathing became shallow and mired with fits of coughing. He kept looking up ahead in hopes of either discovering clean air or at least the source of the smoke.

The winding road up the hill leveled out and expanded into a straight and narrow two-way road. As the forest thinned, the truck accelerated toward civilization. Despite their progress, the smoke was as thick up here as it was down at the lake, and there was no sign of where it was coming from.

Jordan finally broke the silence and asked if Bill knew what was going on with all of the smoke. But he was answered by nothing but silence. Neither the driver nor Bill even bothered looking back at him. Several minutes passed and Jordan shivered, remembering that his life was still at the mercy of these men driving the truck to an unknown destination.

Finally, as they merged onto the interstate, Bill began speaking.

"How do you make a just world, Jordan? How do you suppose peace comes to be? You live in ignorance of the acts that must be performed to maintain equilibrium. Just as your government locks up untold millions, executes hundreds of its own citizens and kills thousands of people in foreign lands, I do my part to maintain balance in my world, my business. I'm no more or less evil than anyone else in this world trying to maintain order. I have killed many men, all for justified reasons. Do you think you are not guilty? Do you think that balance exists between you and I, Jordan? After you defaulted on the line of credit I extended you? After you partnered with an agent of the government trying to bankrupt my entire business? Under which system of justice do you operate?"

Jordan's jaw fidgeted back and forth uncomfortably as he took in everything Bill was saying. He thought it over and acknowledged that he had already admitted this very truth to himself when writing his statement at the police station. But did his crime justify Bill's punishment? Was this truly the only way to achieve peace? After a few minutes had passed, Jordan chose to respond with a question rather than an answer.

"Does being no worse than the government make you a good man?"

"Answer me, Jordan!" Bill responded with agitation, drawing out a pistol and aiming it at Jordan's forehead. His wrinkled, pale-white hand shook as it threatened Jordan's life. Whether the trembling of Bill's hand was from the weight of the gun or a sign of anxiety, Jordan was not sure.

"Your motive is not peace, Bill. You can't justify your actions based on one line of reason when they are executed along another. Furthermore, you take justice into your own hands, no judge and no jury. You break the laws of the land with no regard for the other systems of justice you may be disrupting. In creating your own peace, you are breaking the greater peace of our nation."

"Am I? By killing junkies who don't pay? No one misses them Jordan, don't fool yourself. They were not doing anything good for society. You're the hypocrite here, trying to justify not paying what you owe by standing on some sort of moral high ground. You're no better than me you little fuck."

Bill slammed the butt of the gun across Jordan's face, then turned around and put it away before continuing.

"You work for me, Jordan. Whether you like it or not, you owe me your life. You killed one of my men, you robbed me of ten thousand dollars and you partnered with the police against me. The only reason I haven't killed you already is because you're proving yourself to be more valuable alive than dead at the moment, but have no doubt that I will end you when your value has expired."

Jordan didn't want to live if he had to work for this man, he would rather take his own life. But he still had hope, he still knew there had to be some sort of alternative.

He had already survived longer than he thought he would yesterday. Something must be looking out for him, he thought. He still had hope and was confident that things would not go the way Bill dictated. He kept these thoughts to himself and sat in silence listening as Bill continued to preach.

"Now your friend in the NSA, Rob. Why did he go to Denmark? Your story doesn't add up, he had no reason to flee the NSA, he did nothing wrong."

"He was trying to protect me and Pat. He knew about what we were doing and was obligated to inform his employer. He wanted us to succeed, but was unwilling to do anything more than not turn us in, so he kept silent and left his station to avoid us being found out."

"So he's not loyal to the government? He shares my disdain for their practices and thinks you were justified in your actions? You know, Jordan, you have more in common with me than you care to admit. I could have helped you bring the city down. There are grave injustices committed by this corrupt government. But instead you rebel against them and you rebel against me, so you're left all by yourself." Bill inhaled and began choking on the smoky air, coughing his lungs out and attempting to regain his composure, he eventually continued "I would like to offer you an alliance, a way to right the wrongs you committed against me and a way to further our shared cause against this corrupt institution of the United States. It's a win-win Jordan, all you have to do is give me your word, and let me inject a tracking chip in your neck."

"What good is my word to you if you need to put a

chip in my neck? And what exactly do you want me to do for you in Europe, anyway?"

"You're going to go find Rob, then the two of you will rebuild my empire by starting in Denmark. I will connect you with some product sources there and once you've begun distribution you will send me your profits. Then you will begin bringing product into the US for me and we will finally get that revolution you wanted off the ground. What do you say, Mr. Santarelli?"

A few days ago this would have been a dream come true, but after his dream the previous night Jordan's mind was pre-occupied with thoughts of his mother, Hannah, Ali and William. The love they showed him, the hope he felt when creating art inspired by Hannah, Ali saving his life and offering him honest work, William offering him inspiration and encouragement, he felt guilty even considering turning away from them. When he thought about their philosophy of love, his soul filled with warmth. When he thought of his attempts to bring down the electricity, the Internet and the ideas Bill was now discussing, he felt wretched and sick inside. Yet Jordan knew inside that Bill's offer was actually a demand.

"I don't think I have a choice here, do I?" Jordan responded, not interested in the outcome an upfront refusal might result in.

Bill laughed and nodded, his throaty voice responding in mockery of Jordan's taunt from the previous day, "You always have a choice!"

Jordan sank into his seat, feeling defeated and desperate to get away from Bill.

"At least let me say goodbye to my friends and pack up some of my things first. At least give me that."

Bill remained silent and didn't respond. The truck continued speeding up the interstate, smoke enveloping them from all sides. Jordan took in the silence and began thinking about his dream from the night before, wondering where his mother was, what she was doing, what she might say to him if they found each other. He didn't even know where to start if he wanted to find her, not to mention how he might find Rob if he took on Bill's mission.

Soon the truck exited the freeway and was back on the familiar streets of Seattle. What was not familiar was all the smoke, people walking down the street wearing masks, and the morbid darkness and gloom created by the abundant clouds of ash. As they ascended up Capitol Hill, Jordan recognized his apartment building coming up and felt a rush of relief when the SUV stopped in front of the entrance.

"You have three hours, Jordan. But first we're going to inject this little tracker in your neck."

Jordan's hands clenched tightly into fists and his jaw snapped shut, he had hoped Bill was joking when he first mentioned the tracker, but now it started to seem more real as the man who had been driving the truck joined Jordan in the back and pulled out a briefcase from under the seat.

"This will hurt." the man said, opening the brief case and pulling out a bright silver medical apparatus that looked something like a gun and something like a dental instrument.

The man cleaned Jordan's neck with a sanitary wipe and then held the gun up to his neck. Without warning, Jordan simultaneously heard the loud click of the gun injecting the tracker into his neck and the acute, throbbing pain as if a monster had just bitten his neck. He shrieked and put his hand up to push Bill's accomplice away from him, but the man was strong and resisted. He placed a bandage over Jordan's wound and placed the gun back to the briefcase, sliding it back under the seat and wordlessly returned to the front.

Jordan continued to shriek and clasped his neck in agony as he tried to relieve the pain coursing through him.

"Maybe some dust will help?" Bill said, holding a tray up with a small pile of dust and a cut straw.

Jordan leaned away from the offering, tears running down his face as the pain continued to grow. He knew the dust would relieve his pain, but he had no desire to get hooked after making it through his last withdrawal. He thought of the sweet escape he used to feel when he got high and sighed with desire as he looked at the offering from Bill. But he hated this man, this man was trying to kill him and besides, dust had brought him nothing but misery in the long-term. He couldn't go back to that. Without a word, Jordan opened his door and exited the truck.

"Suit yourself. One o'clock, Jordan. Be here or we'll track you down."

Jordan nodded and slammed the door shut, one hand still grasping his neck with pain. He quickly collapsed to the front stoop of his apartment building and leaned forward, waiting for the pain to die down.

Suddenly a thought burst into his head: He was free. Over the course of the past day he had gone from what felt like certain death to being back in Seattle and free. He was amazed, he could do anything he wanted, at least for a few hours. As he considered his options, he began to cough and choke on the air he was breathing, a dense cloud of smoke had wandered up the hill and made it nearly impossible to breathe.

Standing up, feeling slightly less pain and a desire for cleaner air, Jordan walked into his apartment building.

CHAPTER TWENTY-FIVE

THE FAMILIAR SIGHT OF HIS apartment building was refreshing. Jordan reflected on how many days it had been since he had been home as he walked up the stairs to his unit. Once upstairs, he saw the door to his apartment was ajar. He quickened his step and pushed the door open to see what or who was inside.

As he walked in, his shoes crunched a piece of paper lying on the floor. Picking it up, Jordan read the eviction notice and sighed. It was dated a week ago and informed him he had three days to move out. Laughing with half amusement and half fright, he returned the paper to its place on the floor.

The apartment was empty, entirely vacant. All his furniture was gone, all of his belongings were gone. He walked into the bedroom and saw nothing but recently vacuumed carpet and freshly painted walls. He looked in the closet and there was not a thread in sight. His heart rate quickened as he began thinking of everything that was missing, not so much the furniture or the clothes, but the small things, his most precious possessions that he had kept to ensure he never forgot all the special moments in his life.

Walking into the living room, he felt the blood pump through his veins more quickly, he felt the pounding of his heartbeat against his chest and his ears began to ring with the heightened blood pressure. The pain in his neck returned with a vengeance as he slumped to the floor, leaning his back against a wall where his couch used to be.

His vision blurred and his mind began running rampant, thinking about the statue his mother bought him when they were traveling around Mexico so many years ago, before she moved away. He thought about the journal a friend gave him, filled with messages from his former classmates.

Everything was gone. Vanished. The objects still existed in his memory, but were physically absent from his life. The experiences and people they represented still remained in his mind as well, but now those memories were at greater risk of being entirely forgotten. The totems he had kept to ensure the important moments of his life were never forgotten were all lost.

Also, he had no underwear. Just the clothes on his back. No money to buy new clothes either. The clothes didn't matter so much as the idols, the things of little value to anyone but him and yet taken away for others who will see no meaning in them. Jordan felt his pulse begin to slow down, his heart beating more softly and the ringing in his ears faded. He breathed in the mostly smoke-free air and closed his eyes, telling himself if he made it this far surely he could keep going.

After several minutes passed by, Jordan finally stood up and exited his apartment. When he tried to close the door behind him, he noticed that the lock had been pried off, preventing the door from closing. He left it hanging slightly open just as he had found it. Walking down the stairs he saw the smoke-filled air outside and was eager to find out what was going on. He made his way down to the coffee shop to see who was around.

Entering the store, Jordan saw Ali, Hannah and one other person he didn't recognize working.

"Jordan!" Hannah's voice burst out, as she ran around the counter to greet him with arms spread out for a warm embrace.

Jordan returned Hannah's hug and smiled with joy, he could think back to when no one cared to see him. Even Ali would begrudgingly welcome him to work each day back when he was on dust.

"What happened? How did you get back here?"

"I agreed to work for him, I'm only here to say goodbye. What is with all the smoke?"

Ali finished helping a customer and looked over at Jordan, "You're going to work for that guy? Are you nuts?"

"It's the wildfires, smoke blowing over from eastern Washington, down from Canada and up from Oregon and California. We're surrounded by fires." Hannah answered Jordan's question.

"I don't have much of a choice, Ali. They were ready to kill me, it was the only way I could save my life."

"Don't go back to that life, Jordan." Ali said, shaking his head and going back to help the next customer.

Jordan paused for a moment, considering what he had just heard from Hannah. Wildfires burning from all over, flooding the city with smoke. It was a more powerful message than either of his schemes to disrupt the city had generated, and nature made it happen all on its own. Then his mind turned to Ali's frank advice. Of course he didn't want to work for Bill, and of course he believed he always had a choice. But what was the better option? Flee and play cat and mouse with Bill? The man truly didn't seem afraid to kill him, and now he had a tracker in his neck that made it impossible to hide. Going to Denmark truly felt like his only option, and it carried with it the possibility of finding his mother. Once he was there he didn't have to follow what Bill wanted, for now it was just about getting over there.

"I hung up your drawing, Jordan. It's magnificent!" Hannah exclaimed, changing the topic. She walked over to the far wall and pointed to the framed drawing. She went on, "You have to keep drawing, Jordan. Keep creating, keep spreading the love. No matter where you go. But I pray you will see more options than you see now."

Jordan nodded, he was glad Hannah had seen the drawing he made for her. His gaze shifted to Ali, who seemed to be ignoring him.

"Thanks for saving my life, Ali. And giving me my job back."

Ali paused from his work and looked up at Jordan, his face reflected a mind lost for words. Finally, Ali turned toward the back room and said "Wait."

A few moments later, Ali returned and handed Jordan a check. "For your work. If you come back you still have a job here."

Jordan held the check with gratitude and thanked Ali as he thought of how he might be able to buy some clothes now. Unable to say anything that justified his departure, Jordan simply turned to leave the store.

Hannah shouted, "Your bag!" and approached him holding the sack he had left behind as Bill hauled him out of the store the previous day. It held the drawing supplies Hannah had given him. Taking the bag, Jordan nodded and thanked her.

Guilt slowly crept over him, he didn't feel right leaving behind two of the few people in his life who cared about him. How could he justify his decision to them? He couldn't. Ann would tell him to stay and fight. After being so close to death, Jordan couldn't help but want to get as far from Bill as possible. There was also his dream he had not told anyone about, keeping it closely guarded. The possibility of reuniting with his mother, as impossible as it seemed, motivated him to make the journey abroad.

He looked back at Hannah and Ali, the beautifully painted walls of the shop, art hanging everywhere, including the recent addition of his charcoal drawing. He loved this shop, he loved these people. There were fresh flowers on each table, people sitting and sipping coffee, relaxing music playing over it all. Ali had created a home, a community, Jordan could have been a part of it. He was a part of it, but now he chose to leave.

"I love you guys, I love this store. Thank you for letting me be a part of it." Jordan wasn't changing his decision in spite of this truth and he couldn't think of a more compassionate way to say goodbye. He saw the look of disappointment in Ali's face and the sadness in Hannah's eyes, but proceeded to turn and walk out of the store, returning to the smoke.

Walking up the street toward William's house, the clouds of smoke began to sting Jordan's throat as he breathed them in. Hacking up the polluted air, he struggled to figure out how to breathe in this environment. Surely oxygen would be the next big seller, Jordan thought with sad amusement. He reminisced back to when selling bottled water first became popular and how strange it seemed that people would pay as much for water as they did for soda. Not to mention the more significant implication: water was now under capitalist control.

Jordan covered his mouth with his sleeve and breathed through it, managing to make it a few blocks up the hill. He approached a Money Tree and reluctantly entered, recalling his past visits when he was desperate for a loan to buy some dust before payday. Taking out the check from Ali, he sacrificed ten percent of his pay to get the cash funds. Crossing the street he entered the Goodwill and found some clothes that would fit him as well as a backpack to replace the torn sack he had been carrying around.

"If this doesn't get people to wake up to the reality of Earth's destruction, what will?" the clerk asked , pointing toward the clouds of smoke outside as she rang up Jordan's purchase.

"Love." Jordan replied, surprising himself at the positive attitude that was far from his traditional response.

The clerk shrugged, neither affirming nor rebuking Jordan's assertion. She took his money and gave him a receipt, the beginnings of a smile emerging on her face.

Making his way to William's place, Jordan considered the possibility that William wouldn't be home. It was more likely than not. Nevertheless, he continued making his way across the neighborhood in hopes that he could see his mentor before departing. Unsure how much time had elapsed nor how much time remained before Bill's deadline, Jordan figured that if he was over the agreed upon schedule then Bill would just find him and pick him up anyway, no big deal.

As William's single-story house came into view, Jordan quickened his step, eager to get out of the smoke and hopeful that the lights shining from the window were a sign of William's presence in the home. Knocking on the front door, Jordan was relieved and happy to hear footsteps approach and see William's surprised face as the door creaked open.

"Jordan! Come in, I'll put some tea on."

Jordan entered the living room and took a seat on the familiar, gently worn yellow and tan striped sofa. As the cushions flexed beneath his weight, he felt as if he were sinking into safety. He looked around at the decorations, pictures hanging on the walls, umbrella stand by the door, quilt laid out on top of the adjacent love seat. Sitting on the coffee table in front of him were a handful of photo books, and the framed photos he remembered seeing last time, picturing William alongside his wife and daughter, a smiling, happy family.

"Herbal or black?" William shouted from the kitchen.

Jordan got up and went into the kitchen to respond. He was normally a black tea drinker, but there was something about the home that made him crave a relaxing herbal tea. William's house was a place of peace and serenity, only an herbal tea could compliment that feeling.

After sharing his tea preference with William in the kitchen, he couldn't help but ask the question that had been nagging at him since first seeing the pictures of William's family in the living room, "Where is your family?" Jordan asked as William continued to prepare the tea.

"In heaven, or the afterlife, perhaps reincarnated."

The affirmation of Jordan's suspicion sank in his conscious with a heavy sadness, he had hoped he was wrong.

"I'm sorry. I just saw the photos and…"

"We all die, Jordan." William interrupted.

"Well yeah, but tell me about them."

"Here's your tea, let's go back to the living room." William responded, leading the way.

Jordan followed, sinking back into the living room sofa. There was nothing special about the physical objects in this house, but yet there was an overwhelming mystical essence that Jordan couldn't identify the source of. The last time he remembered feeling this sense of home was in the few memories he still had of his childhood.

"How long have you lived here?"

"Thirty-three years." William responded.

Longer than Jordan had been alive. He thought to himself about what it must be like to live in the same home for so long. Was it even possible for him to do such a thing?

"I still remember when we bought it. Just out of graduate school, both of us, we finally felt like adults. We changed jobs, had kids, there were months we weren't sure how we would pay the mortgage. If you told me I would still be here thirty-three years later it sure would have helped dispel all the fears that welled up in me over the years."

"What happened to them?" Jordan asked, gesturing toward the photos of William's wife and daughter.

"It was a Wednesday. March 9th, 2005. They went to see Bob Dylan at the Paramount. Sheila had never seen him play before, Stella was brimming with excitement to share the cultural icon from our generation with her."

William paused, words failing to continue coming from his mouth. His gaze went down to his feet and his eyes filled with a great sorrow. After a brief pause, William looking unsure how to bring the memories forth into words, he looked up at Jordan and continued.

"I wrote a poem." His breath heavy, he sat up in the rocking chair and cleared his throat before beginning. "The precious stitches take hold and breathe existence into our souls. Becoming part of who we are, stitched together in life, souls unite. When one leaves this universe, the stitches stay strong, the souls remain united. The love grows stronger."

Jordan felt the love in William's heart, the poem led him to reflect on his own life. What souls had he stitched with his own? Had there ever been any? He felt empty.

"A drunk driver. They were on their way home. He hit them head on at fifty miles per hour." William's voice finished the story, the words coming out as if drawn by a higher power, William unable to bring them out on his own.

"I'm sorry, that's awful." Jordan didn't know how to respond to tragedy, he was never able to find the right words. It made him quite uncomfortable. He had no way to express the sorrow he truly felt inside.

William sat back and looked up at the ceiling, sighing

and running his hands down his face. Looking back at Jordan, he took a deep breath and responded, "It was a tragedy, but I still keep their memory with me. So tell me, what have you been up to now? Still trying to destroy modern society?" William asked with a laugh.

"A lot. I actually came by because I wanted to see you before I leave for Denmark."

"Ahh, a socialist paradise! You know they have electricity over there too though, right?" William responded with a grin.

"It's complicated. I don't have much of a choice. I got into debt with my dust dealer and this is the only way to get him off my back."

"You always have a choice, Jordan. And don't be foolish, if you do what he wants then he will always be on your back, breathing down your neck. How much did you get into this guy for?"

"He nearly killed me, William. I am not going to die a martyr. I owe him about ten grand."

"Why not just pay it off then?"

"I am broke. I have a part-time job at a coffee shop making minimum wage. I can barely pay rent and eat. How am I supposed to pay that off?"

"By going to Denmark and becoming an international criminal? Is that the plan, Jordan?"

"It's that or die, and I would prefer to live."

"What if I negotiated a deal and covered your debt?" William asked, raising an eyebrow.

Jordan adjusted himself, feeling uncomfortable and unsure of how to take this proposition. "I couldn't just take your money. Why would you want to do that for me anyway? I would only be transferring my debt from him to you."

"True. But I'm a poetry professor, not a drug lord. Perhaps a better place to have your debt held?"

Jordan nodded. "I don't know how I would pay you back."

"Maybe you need to find a job that pays a little better."

"Like what? I dropped out of high school, if I had stayed I would have flunked out. I have no skills."

"You have a long road ahead of you, and a lot of time, you're young Jordan. Find something you care about, start doing something and getting good at it."

"I'm not going to become another middle-class suit and tie helping destroy the world with Capitalism. Forget it."

"Thank God for that. Becoming a suit is the last thing I would expect of you, Jordan. There are so many other, better options. If you become good at something and put your heart into it, you are bound to produce work that others will value higher than minimum wage. You just have to be willing to do the work."

Jordan re-adjusted himself on the couch in an attempt to ease his inner discomfort, then he looked down at the carpet. He was conflicted. It was clear from his encounters with Ali, Hannah and William that staying in Seattle was the right thing to do. So why was he still drawn to Denmark? Was it a hope of settling things with Bill? The possibility of seeking out his mother? Escape? Or was there something else? Perhaps it was the excitement of an adventure, a new place, and a better society that were all pulling him toward the onward journey.

"I had a dream last night. It reminded me of my mother and how disconnected we are. She moved to Europe after I was out of the house and I haven't seen her since. I think if I go to Denmark, I might be able to find her." Jordan looked up from the carpet to see William's response.

William nodded, "I see you're not entirely evil, Jordan. Family is worth fighting for, but you must be honest with yourself if that's your aim. You're not giving in and working for your drug dealer because you have no choice. You're taking advantage of the drug dealer whom you have already taken advantage of by not paying him back. You're using him to get to Europe so that you can seek out your Mom. Can you accept that truth?"

Jordan stood up and straightened out his pants, feeling unable to sit comfortably anymore, he sat back down again after re-arranging the pillows behind him. He knew William was speaking the truth, but Jordan still felt a sense of helplessness in the situation. He was the victim, not the attacker, yet the way William put it, he didn't sound like a victim at all. He just wanted to do the right thing, but no one was telling him what the right thing to do was. Were they? He thought back to what Ali, Hannah and now William all were telling him: Stay. Why was this solution so hard to accept? Why didn't what others felt the right thing to do was feel right to him?

One thing was certain: he didn't want to die. Staying here, being so close to Bill, and not doing what Bill wanted, seemed like it could only result in certain death to him. Paying back his debt was impossible, and while William offered a compelling financing plan, taking flight to Denmark just seemed so much more peaceful, eloquent, relaxed. His mother wasn't just an excuse, he really desired to re-connect and see if he could regain that sense of family he felt so deprived of, that sense of love he felt in his dream.

"If it's really the truth, then I have no choice but to accept it whether I like it or not. What if there are more possibilities than you and I have been able to come up with though? Maybe I can find a way to keep my word with Bill."

"I just hope you don't end up in jail, Jordan. Be careful out there." William said, ending the discussion and not interested in attempting any further persuasion.

Jordan nodded, disappointed not to have received an endorsement for his plan from anyone he visited. All the people he had missed so desperately while in the holding cell and tied up at Bill's cabin, they all cared about him, he was sure of that, but none of them supported his decision. In fact, they all argued for reversing course. He wondered what it was in him that was so defiant, so convinced he was right and they were wrong.

A fist knocked heavily on the front door. Jordan leaped up in fear, sure that whoever was on the other side of the door was looking for him. William stood up and asked Jordan "Expecting company?"

"No, but I'm sure whoever it is, is here for me."

William opened the door and revealed Bill standing outside, his face looked stern and displeased. Behind Bill stood the unnamed driver, expressionless, emotionless, robotic.

"You're late. You could have missed your flight if we didn't track you down." Bill said.

"I'm sorry, I don't have a phone, or a watch. I lost track of time. I figured you would find me in any case."

William looked perturbed, biting his lip and slowly staring back and forth between Bill and Jordan, he nodded with understanding of what was going on. "I'll be seeing you then, Jordan." he said, gesturing with his arm out the door for Jordan to depart.

Jordan nodded, walked to the door and paused before stepping across the threshold to look at William in the eyes. "I'll be honest with myself, I promise."

William was clearly not pleased, and only acknowledged Jordan with a slight nod while his arm was still leading Jordan out of the house.

"Get in the truck." Bill instructed. As Jordan walked toward the familiar idling black SUV, he felt a pang of guilt, but an equally brilliant burst of hope.

CHAPTER TWENTY-SIX

As the jet descended toward Copenhagen, Jordan envied the Russian man passed out in the seat next to him. The past twelve hours of travel had completely exhausted him, he had been unable to get a wink of sleep and was too tired to coherently follow any of the entertainment available to watch on the mediatron mounted in front of him. Jordan was now in a zombie-like state, having been awake for over twenty-four hours and longing desperately for a bed. His mind had been racing since he arrived at the airport in Seattle, wondering how he would get through security with the tracking chip in his neck, and whether the lie detectors at immigration would catch him.

Yet here he was, landing in Copenhagen, unsure how he would go about finding Rob or his mother. All he had were some clothes and a few dollars leftover from the paycheck he cashed before he left. Bill told him someone would be at the airport waiting to pick him up. Jordan wasn't sure if he wanted to seek out his welcoming party or avoid them.

Passing through immigration couldn't have been easier, they didn't say a word to him, only took his passport, looked at him, stamped it and returned the passport. Security was a similarly smooth experience, the implant apparently not containing enough metal to set off the metal detector. As Jordan departed the secured portion of the airport, he saw a handful of men in suits, each carrying a sign with a different name. Sure enough there was one that read "Santarelli." He realized that he could keep walking and leave Bill and his scheme behind him, but how would he get by? He had hardly any money and nowhere to stay. He approached the man holding his sign and decided to see where following Bill's plan would lead him.

"Jordan, is it?" The man holding the sign asked.

"Yeah, that's me."

"Your bags?"

"This is it." Jordan responded, gesturing to the ruck sack on his back.

"Alright then. Let's go."

The man led Jordan out to an idling black town car. Why were the vehicles of his drug overlords always black, Jordan pondered. It was as if businessmen and the criminal underworld both conspired to be devoid of creative energy.

When he sat in the back seat of the sedan, he saw that there were two men already sitting in the car, one in the back seat next to Jordan and the other in the passenger seat up front. Once the driver took his place, there were three suits and Jordan.

"Where to, boys?" Jordan asked in a dreary voice attempting to lighten the mood while struggling to function in his zombie-like state.

"We're going to the house. You need to get some rest." Said the man sitting in front of him, with a thick Scandinavian accent.

The car accelerated and left the airport in a hurry. Jordan looked out the window, still unable to fall asleep. He closed his eyes, but his mind continued to race. Were these people Bill's employees, or just business partners? Were they as cruel and evil as Bill? Where was "the house"? Where was Rob? Where was his mom?

Jordan opened his eyes. The countryside was beautiful. He saw fields of green stretching out for miles and wondered what crops were being grown. Surely the vegetables and grain for the region must come from these plants. Miles and miles of food growing out in the open air. It was so easy to forget that such places existed when you spent every day in a city. Seeing the fields led Jordan to question where it all came from? The food, the cars, the sidewalks? Everything in the city came from the outside. What was created within? The information, the cooking, the art. Did a city sit at the pinnacle of civilization? A peak that wouldn't exist without the sustenance provided by the people out here, the people of the land.

They continued driving, fields kept passing by. Trees occasionally grew, slightly different looking than the trees back home. Sheep. Fences. The road seemed to have no end. They were the only town car in sight. Sleep was necessary.

The house was a stone house, two stories tall, modest in dimensions. Ordinary. They parked alongside the house and Jordan saw a tree in the back yard, leafy with fruit hanging from the branches. Smoke wafted from the chimney. Lights shone on inside. Jordan's door opened. A man blocked his exit. The man had a wand. Magical wand? The wand went to his neck. The wand chirped. The man looked at the chirp and read the wand. The man nodded and made way for Jordan to depart the town car.

Jordan was tired. He felt as if he might collapse at any moment. Thinking was hard. Walking was even more challenging. He followed the men into the house and saw a woman in the kitchen. He saw stairs, narrow, like a ship, leading up and up to somewhere up there.

Walking up the stairs he saw a door, it had a knob that turned and when it turned the door gave way and there was a bed inside. The man who had followed him up told him to sleep and closed the door behind him. The latch locked, it locked from the wrong side. Jordan didn't care because there was a bed.

CHAPTER
TWENTY-SEVEN

W HEN JORDAN AWOKE, THE SUN was shining bright through the curtains covering the window in his bedroom. The wind blew in and the curtains rose as they submitted to the morning breeze, he could hear birds chirping outside. Feeling well-rested and rejuvenated, Jordan leapt out of bed and slid the curtains aside to look out at his surroundings. The window revealed a lush emerald landscape covered in grasses with trees scattered throughout rolling hills. He breathed in the fresh air, pure and refreshing, it was a great relief to be free from the smoke-filled air he had left behind in Seattle.

The house was quiet, not a sound emerged from outside his door or beneath his feet. Jordan remembered the click of the door locking him in the room before he had fallen asleep and cautiously approached the door to see whether he was locked in to the room. As he turned the handle the door freed itself from the latch and opened, surprising Jordan and revealing the narrow staircase down to the main living area of the house.

Stepping out onto the landing, Jordan sought out a bathroom with hopes of taking a shower. He opened the door adjacent to his bedroom and found a sparkling clean bathroom awaiting him. The shower was warm, the water was soft, Jordan could have stayed under the stream pouring down and cleansing his body for hours. After he felt thoroughly refreshed, he exited and discovered a towel as well as a change of clothes sitting on the counter. This house felt more like a resort than a drug haven.

Dressed and curious if anyone was around, Jordan walked downstairs to the ground floor. He scanned the house, but didn't see any signs of life. The kitchen, living room and library were all vacant. Wandering outside, he felt the cool morning breeze and warm sunshine grace his skin and breathed in the crisp, fresh air. What a place, he thought. He felt alive, he felt energized and more vibrant than he had felt in years, he couldn't remember the last time he felt like this.

The absence of people was surprising, confusing and slightly disturbing. As Jordan walked around the house he did not see the town car that had dropped him off. The road that ran past the house must have been a rural one, no cars were passing by and there were no other houses in sight. Where was everyone? With no way to contact his hosts, Jordan wandered through the fields surrounding the house and took a seat under the shade of a rather large apple tree, leaning up against the trunk and staring out across the field toward the house.

How to find Rob, how to find his Mother, how to begin working for these drug dealers. These questions spun through his mind, unsure where he could even start. Time was of the essence, yet there wasn't a thing he could do and it was rather comforting to just sit and enjoy this peaceful moment.

The lawnmower-esque whirr of a car making its way toward the house caught Jordan's attention. The car was a compact, light-blue hatchback covered in dust and the buildup that comes along with years without a car wash. Slowing down as it approached the driveway, the car turned in and came to a stop in front of the house. Jordan stayed seated, observing the scene with interest.

While the car remained idling, the driver's side door opened and a middle-aged man in a black leather jacket and blue jeans stepped out. The man's hair was black with streaks of grey, cut short enough that it stood up with minimal assistance from styling gel. As the man approached the house he knock on the front door, indicating to Jordan that he must be a visitor and not his new employer.

The man appeared unarmed and harmless enough that Jordan decided to approach him and inquire. As he walked over from the apple tree, Jordan caught the man's attention.

"Jordan? Is that you?" The man shouted.

Unsure how or whether to respond and alarmed to hear his own name from the stranger, Jordan remained silent and continued approaching, squinting to try and get a better look at the man.

"Jordan, it's me. It's Rob. Do you remember me?"

"Rob? Do you work with these guys? How did you find me?"

"No, we need to talk. Want to go for a drive?"

Jordan was excited and relieved that Rob had somehow

managed to find him, but unsure of his methods and suspect of his allegiances. He looked at Rob, now that he was close enough to make out his expression. The man in front of him barely resembled the man he remembered from back in Seattle. He looked happy and free, hopeful and unburdened. There was something about his voice and his demeanor that led Jordan to give him a chance.

As the car departed the driveway and turned on to the road, Jordan was glad to be sitting in the front seat of a regular car for once. He rolled down his window, manually, and basked in the Scandinavian air.

"I found you because of the tracking chip they planted in you. You do know you're broadcasting your location wherever you go, right?"

Jordan nodded with a sigh of understanding. Of course Rob tracked him down with his NSA sleuthing skills. But Jordan was curious how exactly he managed to di t. He asked Rob for an explanation, "How?"

"Not that many people with tracking chips flying into Copenhagen, when I saw the signal and checked the inbound flight records I knew there was a good chance of it being you."

"So can you remove the tracker?"

"I'm not a surgeon, Jordan. And I'm not interested in helping you before I know more about who exactly you're working for and why you're over here."

"I don't really know who I'm working for. They picked me up at the airport and took me to the house, but when I woke up they were gone."

"Well, they don't need to be physically present to keep

an eye on you with that tracking device. They may be chasing us down as we speak."

"What are you doing here, Rob? Undercover for the NSA?"

"Hah! I'm on the run, kid. There's no easy way to leave the NSA, this was the most harmless route I could come up with."

"So what do you do over here?"

"This and that. I help people leave the intelligence business and also work with some of the activists here to prevent the EU from following in America's footsteps."

"Where are we going?"

"Into the city. You still haven't told me why you came here."

Jordan considered whether to tell Rob the full story of Bill's plan to have the two of them work together. His distaste for everything about Bill, combined with the physical distance that was now between them and the absence of his new hosts inclined him to just forget the whole deal and focus on finding his mother. But then William's words replayed in his head and he felt obligated to repay his debt to Bill if he could.

"I was sent here by a drug dealer I owe money to back home. He wanted me to meet up with you and start a distribution and sales business over here, sending our profits back to him."

"Wow, I thought you were just a cyber-terrorist, now you're telling me you're in the drug business too? How did your boss know about me? And what did he think I would do for you?"

"I was desperate. He had me tied up and was about to

drown me. I told him everything I thought might save my life, including the NSA agent I met who fled to Denmark when I told him what I had done with the Internet, you."

"And he expected me to do what for you? Voluntarily?"

"Smuggle dust back into the US."

Rob burst out with laughter before Jordan could say another word.

"Not a chance, Jordan."

"I know, I can see how absurd of an idea it is now that I've said it to you. I didn't even think I would find you over here. But you wanted to know why I was here, now you know."

"Well, I want you to meet some friends of mine who might have some better ideas for you. Unless you want me to take you back to the house? I'm not going to be helping you with any sort of drug distribution or transportation, so you can forget about that."

Jordan slouched in his seat. The idea actually had made sense to him when Bill suggested it, but now it seemed entirely foolish. How was he supposed to repay Bill if he didn't do this deal? Were some Danish drug dealers hot on his trail now? Would they kill him for fleeing? Why was his life constantly fucked?

"Sure, I'll meet your friends. Why not?"

As the car entered the city of Copenhagen, Jordan was shocked by the swarms of bicyclists riding past on both sides of the road. There had to be more bikes than cars out here. The city was beautiful, buildings that must have been standing for centuries lined the streets, the sidewalks were clean, and every few blocks a magnificently landscaped park passed by. The bicyclists were not the rabid pseudo-racers that he was used to seeing whizz around Seattle. No, these were just everyday people, sitting up straight and riding with grace and a smile. They wore regular clothes and traveled at a speed that made a helmet unnecessary. The cars were not whizzing around each other and honking, people just seemed to be getting along with each other and going with the flow.

Rob parked the car in front of a nondescript building with a few people standing outside and smoking. As they entered the building, the smokers greeted Rob in Danish. Walking through the entryway revealed a warehouse-like interior with a tall metallic ceiling and drab walls with large square windows along the top. Ceiling fans hung down and spun slowly, cutting through the light shining from overhead flood lamps. If it wasn't for the colorful artwork hanging on the walls, the place would have given off a bit of an eery vibe, instead Jordan felt a warmth as he saw the people congregating around tables and talking energetically, all in incomprehensible Danish.

"Velkommen til folkets hus!" said a man with arm outstretched in greeting to Jordan.

Jordan looked to Rob for a translation.

"He says welcome, is it really that hard to understand? Shake his hand."

Jordan returned his gaze to the man and shook his hand, not saying a word.

Rob resolved the situation by responding to the man, "My friend doesn't speak Danish."

"Ah, welcome to the people's house…American?"

Jordan nodded, relieved to hear a language he understood. "Yes, from Seattle. Is this where the communists gather to conspire against the oppressors?"

Rob and the Danish man broke out in laughter, then the Dane responded "Not exactly, although some have done that here. This is a cafe. Would you like a drink?"

"Sure." Jordan responded, following the man to the bar with Rob.

As the three sat down at a table after ordering their drinks, the Dane was the first to speak up.

"My name is Hans. I was born out in the country, but call Copenhagen home now. How do you know Rob?"

"We met through a mutual acquaintance back in Seattle. I was recruiting Rob to help me with a ...project, but he ended up flying out here instead."

Jordan was unsure how much Hans knew about Rob, what was a secret and what was safe to say. Were these people fighting the government, or just hanging out? He had never been to a place like this before. Was it just a drab cafe, or was there more to it?

Rob continued where Jordan had left off, "Jordan came here to distribute drugs in an attempt to pay off a debt he owes to a drug dealer back in America. Maybe you could work with him?"

Jordan was shocked, he felt bare and exposed, as if Rob had just stripped him of his clothing and he was now naked in front of Hans and anyone else in the cafe who may have overheard. Looking around for reactions, he saw none. Hans only nodded and smiled before he responded.

"The drugs are illegal here, they are also not very popular. You will have a tough market. Be careful."

Rob interrupted, "You should check out Christiania. They have a decent pot market."

Jordan felt as if he was carrying on an act and he was tired of playing the part. If Rob wasn't going to give him any insider access, his hosts had abandoned him and he was really just trying to repay Bill in the first place, with no motive to join the drug profession, then why was he acting as if that was his true motive?

"I'm actually here to find my mom." He admitted.

Rob and Hans both stared at Jordan without immediately responding. The admission seemed to have caught them off-guard. Jordan felt a sudden and unexpected wave of relief run through his body, unsure why he ever kept his additional motive for coming to Europe a secret. While his companions continued to stare at him questioningly, Jordan continued.

"I don't know where she is. We lost touch when she moved out here over ten years ago and I chose not to go with her. I thought she was nuts and was leaving to get away from me. We haven't spoken since."

"Wow, now that's a story. How will you find her?" Hans responded, leaning forward and suddenly taking an interest in Jordan.

"Now there's something I might be able to help you with." Rob chimed in.

Jordan smiled as he briefly reflected on how strangely events had unfolded so far on his first day in Copenhagen. Despite his willingness and effort to be complicit with Bill's plan, nothing was getting off the ground. Yet after speaking just one explanatory sentence about his search for his mother and capturing the interest of two companions, he felt immensely hopeful that his real quest, the one closest to his heart may prove fruitful. Unsure how to express his gratitude to Rob, Jordan paused and simply said "Thank you."

At that moment, a man walked through the entrance of the cafe and gained the attention and silence of the patrons simply by the threads covering his body. The finely pressed suit, neatly tied tie and slicked-back haircut set the man apart from everyone else in the cafe. As Jordan looked on, he knew the man had come here for him. Without a word, he stood up and walked toward the suit. Rob and Hans remained seated and watched the scene unfold with disdain.

"Come back soon, Jordan!" Hans shouted.

CHAPTER TWENTY-EIGHT

THE SEDAN PAINTED WITH A glossy black finish and silver trim was all too familiar. Jordan took his seat in the back, he was depressed that the man had showed up, but eager to get some answers about exactly what they were doing here, and what they expected from him. But as the man who came to get him took his seat in front, he spoke up before Jordan could ask any questions.

"You found your way into the city, eh? Friends here?"

Unwilling to be a submissive lackey, Jordan responded with his own questions.

"Where did you all go? The house was empty this morning. Did you just expect me to sit around?"

"We had some business to attend to and thought you would sleep in later than you did."

Feeling on slightly more level, yet still unequal footing with his new oppressors, Jordan responded to their inquiry.

"Yes, I have friends here. How do you sell drugs here if no one wants them?"

"We focus on export."

Jordan sighed, his delusion that this organization might not be as built-up as Bill's used to be back home.

"What do you want me to do here?" He asked.

"it's simple, Jordan. You will help us get our products into America. Your fellow Americans seem to love dust and our other products more than any other country, did you know that? Perhaps getting high is the real American dream?"

Jordan laughed and a smile burst onto his face. "Yes, life is pretty miserable in America and getting a little high is the only way some people can get by."

"Good then, we'll go back to the house and show you how to swallow packages."

Jordan's smile disappeared and the image of the fat woman in the back of the van and Victor prepping a needle injection to get him hard flashed through his mind. He was disgusted, both with the idea of smuggling drugs by using his body as a storage mechanism and with himself for being in a situation where others expected him to be open to such an idea.

Staring out the window, Jordan thought of how he might escape. There surely had to be a better way to repay his debt than to swallow condoms full of dust Risking his life, risking becoming an international criminal, this was just too much. He already knew there was a better way, William had put it right in front of him: transfer the debt to a sane person, work it off, over time. He wished he had taken the offer. Being in this car, with these men, asked to complete an inhuman act was just as bad as being tied up on Bill's dock.

Jordan suddenly felt sick, his stomach churned and

his forehead beaded with sweat. He rolled down the window and leaned his head out. The fresh air helped, but he still felt as if he might vomit at any moment. Then he wondered why he cared to keep his vomit off the interior of these men's car. He pulled his head back inside and leaned toward the empty seat next to him. His nausea grew more intense and a moment later vomit made its way up his throat and onto the previously clean black leather upholstery of the car.

"Godshit fuck!" exclaimed the man seated in front of Jordan. "Pull over!" he ordered the driver.

As the car pulled to the side of the road, Jordan opened his door and stood over the grass strip that ran along the thoroughfare they had been driving on. He no longer felt sick, but he had no desire to re-enter the car that now reeked of his vomit and was bound for a journey he had no desire of continuing. He watched the nameless suit who had been speaking to him step out of the car.

"No!" Jordan exclaimed. "I'm not going to do it. You will have to find another drug mule."

"You don't have a choice in the matter." The man responded, pulling his blazer aside to reveal a silver pistol strapped to his belt.

Jordan stared out at the oncoming traffic. They were still in the outskirts of the city. He saw no escape, but would die before he got back into the car. Walking up toward the suit, he stared into the man's eyes, tired of running and tired of being controlled, he kept his head up and stopped only when his forehead was inches from the suit's. Gun drawn, the suit stared back at Jordan and ordered him back into the car.

"No." Jordan simply responded, pressing his forehead against the suit's and staring into his eyes with the conviction to no longer be a pawn and comply. "I will repay my debt to Bill. But not like this."

The suit took a step back and holstered his gun. "Bill will kill you." he said.

Jordan looked on and shrugged, continuing to stare into the eyes of the suit. "Come what may, I'm not going to do what you say."

The suit nodded and turned away from Jordan, walking toward the car. Jordan watched as the sedan drove off, continuing toward the house without him. He felt that same sense of relief he had felt when he told Hans and Rob his true reason for coming to Europe.

The traffic continued to flow by, Jordan looked back toward the city and began walking down the grass running along the highway. Was he free now? The threat of Bill still loomed, but he was so far away, what could he possibly do from such a distance? There was still a tracker in his neck and music to face when he returned home, if he returned home. Jordan's thoughts turned toward his mother, unsure where to even begin in the search for her, his only hope was the expertise and help from Rob and possibly Hans.

After walking nearly a mile back toward the city a car slowed down as it passed by Jordan and pulled off into the shoulder. Jordan turned around and recognized Rob's dust-covered blue hatchback idling. He ran over and saw Hans exiting the passenger seat to greet him. As the two met, Jordan felt an electric surge of joy and hope rush through his bones.

"We tracked you!" Hans announced.

Jordan laughed, "This chip in my neck is proving more helpful than I ever imagined."

"Fancy a lift?" Rob asked, shouting from the driver's seat.

Jordan nodded and climbed into the backseat of the car. As they pulled back into traffic, Rob took the next turnaround and drove back toward Copenhagen.

"So what happened? Whisked away by the criminal underworld one minute and walking along the shoulder of the highway the next. Did you kill them?"

"No, not even close. I was just lucky." Jordan didn't want to talk about the drug cartel anymore, he was done with them and the less he talked about them the sooner he hoped they would leave his thoughts. Changing the subject, he continued "Will you help me track down my mother?"

"Of course!" Hans chimed in before Rob could respond. "There's a big festival at the park tonight. Maybe she'll be there!" he added.

"Whats her name?" Rob asked, with considerably less enthusiasm than Hans.

"Jane. Jane Santarelli. Or at least that was the surname she took from my father. She could have changed it, remarried, who knows."

"Well, not a lot of Santarelli's in Denmark. I'll start looking around online tonight."

"If she's not at the picnic!" Hans responded with his eternal positivity.

"I'm not even sure if she's in Denmark. It's been twelve

years since we spoke and when she left it wasn't clear exactly where she planned on landing." Jordan lamented.

"God works in mysterious ways, we will find her, have faith, Jordan!" Hans went on with his relentless optimism.

The three journeyed back into the city and spent the afternoon at Hans' house preparing a picnic dinner for the festival. Jordan felt a strange sense of remorse, wishing he had just stayed home. What was he doing out here? He had no money, a slim chance of finding his mother. He was grateful for the friendship of Hans and Rob, but he missed the friendships he had just begun growing back home. He didn't want to start over.

Hans had a nice home, it reminded Jordan of William's place back in Seattle. It felt warm, safe, cozy. Hans had clearly dwelled in the small, somewhat cramped one bedroom flat for a while. Unlike William's place, there were no photos of family or kids to be seen, but Hans was young and couldn't have been more than a handful of years out of college.

They were able to walk to the park, only about a mile from Hans' place. As they entered through the tall iron gate, Jordan was awestruck by how beautiful the park was. People would be charged admission to visit such a magnificent place back in America. The park extended for blocks, full of lush green grass terraces with big willow trees providing shade for all the people peppered around enjoying themselves. There was a large lake in the center, flat as a pancake and reflecting the surrounding people and foliage.

At the far end of the park a few people were hard at work assembling a small stage. The sun still hung well above the buildings that surrounded them and Hans led the way to a clearing in the shade with a view of the stage.

"There will be music? This is all free?" Inquired Jordan.

"Yes, several bands. There's always music in Copenhagen. Tonight is a local group, they will probably play some American covers!"

Jordan laid back in the grass and stared up at the tree branches hanging overhead. He took a deep breath, the air felt so clean and pure here. This park felt like paradise, and Jordan was simply grateful to be alive, free and outside. What a feeling, what a gift. He thought of his friends back home and wished they were here with him, he knew they would love it. Closing his eyes he pictured Hannah in his mind's eye, working at the coffee shop, or was she at home? Writing, drawing? Defying all the negative energy around her and in the process redirecting it to help spread good, slowly building a fearless army of love and hope.

"Jordan, wake up! Let's go find your mum!" Hans voice interrupted the daydream and Jordan returned to reality, which wasn't as scary as it usually was for once.

Standing up, the two left Rob alone setting up their dinner. They began to slowly walk back and forth, criss-crossing the terraced hill. After a few journeys back and forth Hans asked Jordan "What does she look like? Seen anyone close yet?"

"Not quite as tall as I am. Short, dark hair. Or at least it was short when she left. She wore glasses. Has to be in her sixties by now."

The two finished covering one quadrant of the park and moved on to the next, slowly making their way up the terrace. Jordan looked on searching for his mother, seeing mostly younger Danish couples enjoying their afternoon in the park. Ahead, Jordan saw an older woman sitting alone, he examined her facial features and tried to discern whether it was his mother. She had long, dark hair with traces of grey, wrinkled skin and wore glasses, looking out over the lake as she sipped a glass of wine. As they got closer, Jordan opened his mouth, then closed it unsure of exactly what to say.

Finally, determined to say something, Jordan stopped walking a few paces in front of the woman and asked "Jane? Are you Jane?"

The woman looked up and shook her head, "No." she responded with a sympathetic look on her face.

Jordan nodded and turned away, his face flush with embarrassment. The two continued wandering up and down the terraces until they made their way around the entire park. Jordan didn't expect to find her here, it would have been too easy. At the same time, he was disappointed. The more he thought about his mother the more he missed her. He wished they had stayed in touch. He truly wanted to find her.

Sitting back down with Rob, the three ate their dinner and watched the sunset. Without a word they took it all in, hearing the band begin to play down on the stage and enjoying the food they had prepared. The air was filled with the smell of others' smoking barbecues, trees and a hint of ocean breeze. Jordan breathed it all in and felt hopeful.

CHAPTER TWENTY-NINE

THE MORNING SUNLIGHT SHONE IN through the open windows above the couch in Hans' living room where Jordan had spent the night. Jordan slowly awoke and saw an acoustic guitar on a stand next to an aging brown recliner across the room from him. As he remained laying on the couch staring at the guitar, its strings glistening in the sunlight, he thought over his present dilemma.

How on earth was he going to find his mother? He still remembered the dream he had while laying on the dock outside Bill's cabin. He recalled the feeling of love and the warming of his heart that he had experienced during the dream and had remained with him upon awakening, but had slowly been fading ever since. He tried as hard as he could to hold on to the warmth, but it continued to slip out of his heart and mind with each passing day.

His only hope of finding his mother was either through Rob's technological wizardry or pure random chance. Jordan didn't have much faith in random chance and so he hoped that somehow Rob would be able to work his magic and find her.

The others were still asleep, the house was silent aside

from the birds singing their morning songs outside. The couch had been surprisingly comfortable to sleep on and Jordan thought of just laying there in contemplative agony until the others awoke. No, he decided. He was determined to get his mind off of his troubles.

Righting himself and glancing around the house he thought about how much more welcoming and homely Hans' place felt compared with the drug ring's house he had slept in the previous night. It wasn't as clean and neat here, but yet it was much more comfortable. Jordan walked out of the flat and down the spiral staircase to exit the building.

The city was slowly coming to life, shop clerks swept the entrances to their stores in the crisp morning air, people were walking in all directions and an occasional bicycle or motorcycle passed by on the road. After wandering aimlessly for a few minutes, Jordan arrived at a park, it was not as big as the one they had gone to last night, but it was no less elegant and well maintained. Beautiful paving stones lined the walkway, surrounded by neatly trimmed shrubs and all sorts of different trees. In the center of the park stood a fountain with a statue in the middle.

Jordan thought about what it would take to get a statue of his likeness in the center of a park. Most people never got that far in life, he certainly wasn't anywhere near the mark. He wondered what this man had done, was he a politician, an artist, a warrior? Who knew, Jordan didn't care enough to read the placard with the answer.

As he wandered the park he saw others walking through, weaving across the park on their way to whatever they happened to be doing that day. None of them resembled his mother. He sat on a bench along the walkway that circled the fountain. As he watched the people walk by, he tried to bring back that feeling of love that was fading from his heart. Closing his eyes, he tried to remember the dream, the warmth, and re-create what he had felt. He thought of his mother and recalled the limited memories he had of his childhood growing up with her. He was more determined than ever to find her, to rebuild that lost feeling and be part of a family once again.

He thought he heard someone nearby say his name, opening his eyes he saw a couple walking by, talking with each other, they waved a brief greeting to Jordan as they passed by. Jordan sighed, discouraged. This attempt to find his mother by dumb luck was absolutely hopeless, sitting around and hoping his mother would pass by was a waste of time. Jordan resumed walking and headed back toward Hans' place thinking the others might be awake by now.

As he entered the flat, he heard the clang of dishes coming from the kitchen. Wandering in, he saw Hans' at work on the grill.

"Good morning!" Jordan announced, saliva beginning to flow in his mouth as the smell of roasted potatoes and fried eggs wafted toward him.

"Hey Jordan, I saw you were up and out the door when I woke up. Eggs?" Hans asked in greeting.

"Yes, please."

Rob was sitting in the living room strumming Hans'

guitar, attempting to play a song but failing to keep up after three or four bars.

"Jordan, I started looking for a Jane Santarelli last night. No exact matches here in Denmark, but there are a few Santarellis. I can get you their details."

"Did you find a Jane Santarelli outside Denmark?"

"Oh, a few in Italy and Greece you know. But all cross-referenced with EU passports so unlikely to be your mum. I got a hit in England, think she may have landed in London?"

"Quite possibly, she didn't speak any languages other than English, so England would make sense. Do you have a phone number?"

"Not yet, but I'll see what I can find on that one after breakfast."

Jordan thought about what his mother might be doing in London. Was she working? Married? An artist? Had she found the happiness she was looking for? Was she a celebrity now? For the moment he thought of her as a real person again, rather than the mystery in his mind she had been for the past decade. Did she remember him? Would she be glad to hear from him? He wanted to make the phone call today and find out whether this woman in London was in fact his mother.

After rushing through breakfast, Jordan stood eagerly over Rob's shoulder as he flipped through various websites and terminal windows on his laptop.

"She's not in any public phone listings. All I can find is a house address."

"Does she have a mobile?"

"If she does, it's not under her name. You're probably best off writing a letter."

"Writing a letter? Sending it in the mail? And then what, sit around and wait for a response?" Jordan couldn't fathom waiting that amount of time. He wanted to go to her door right away.

"Fly then?" Hans asked, joining the conversation.

Jordan looked at his feet, he was down to just a few dollars, not enough for a plane ticket, not enough to do hardly anything. He had his return ticket back home that Bill had given him before he departed, it was dated for a month from his arrival, when he presumably would make his first smuggling run. He thought about whether he could somehow use the value of the ticket to get to London, but as he was considering this option Hans continued.

"I know! Let's drive! C'mon, it'll be fun!" Hans chirped with enthusiasm.

Jordan looked at Hans to see if he was serious, then he looked to Rob for a reaction. Rob's face was muted, expressionless.

"I have the cash, I can get you on a SleazyJet over to London. Don't worry about driving." Rob responded.

"No, I don't want your money. I already have enough debt."

"It's a fifteen hour drive, you've gotta be nuts to go for that. The cost of gas alone is the same as a plane ticket. Just fly over." Rob rebutted.

"Road trip!" Hans interjected encouragingly.

Jordan reached in his pocket and pulled out his remaining cash, handing it over to Hans and answering, "This is all I have."

"No, keep it. This is going to be fun! You coming Rob?" Hans asked with enthusiasm.

Rob looked around the house, and back at Hans and Jordan. He shrugged his shoulders and responded with an indecisive, "I guess."

"Great, bring the guitar too!" Hans said.

The three piled into Hans' white station wagon with Hans taking the driver's seat, Jordan up front and Rob in the back tuning the guitar.

"I bet we can make it in fourteen hours, what do you think?" Hans questioned as he sped out of the driveway through the streets of Copenhagen toward the highway.

Jordan smiled without responding. He stared out at the open road and thought how lucky he was to have found Rob, or rather for Rob to have found him. And now he had Hans' aid as well, neither of these two were under any obligation to help him, yet here they were. Hans reminded him of Hannah, eternally optimistic, smiling and helpful. He wished he could be like them, but it was hard to even try. When he did put forth an effort, it felt inauthentic. How could one be aware of all the problems in this world, all the evil and all the people acting to make it worse instead of better, but smile anyway? Were they faking ignorance? Jordan had no interest in being fake, but believed there must be something that laid beyond his understanding to explain how genuine Hans and Hannah acted despite all the ruin around them.

To be positive in the face of such evil, to know things were awful and wrong and so many people were only making it worse by their inaction, and respond simply by smiling at everyone and extend a helping hand was unfathomable to Jordan. This amount of love seemed beyond reach, yet he knew that obtaining and spreading it was his only hope of making the world a better place.

"Teach me, Hans." He said.

"Teach you what? Guitar? I can't do that and drive."

"Not good enough for you, eh?" Rob responded, strumming random chords on the guitar in the backseat.

"No, teach me how to be happy. You're always so happy. Do you just ignore everything that's wrong with the world? How do you do it?"

"I don't ignore anything, Jordan! I just can't think of a better way to respond to it all than with love. You respond with anger and does that make things better? No, it makes them worse. Now everything sucks and you're in a bad mood."

"Sure, I would love to be happy. I would do anything for it. I've read dozens of self-help books. I've tried to fake it, but the bitterness of the world always comes back to the forefront of my mind and I can't help but be overcome with anger and sorrow."

"Well, it takes more than a positive attitude, Jordan. You've also got to take some positive actions. What are you doing to make the world a better place?"

"Uhh, helping the drug underworld? I don't know. What do you do?"

"I work at the cafe, I let ex-spies from the US stay at my flat, sometimes I even give depressed drug smugglers rides to London."

Jordan smiled and let a laugh jump from his mouth. Then his thoughts turned to the past few days, and how people were always helping him, but he was never helping anyone. It wasn't his fault, was it? When did people come to him for help? If they did, he would help, truly he would.

"No one ever needs my help though." He responded, feeling righteously exceptional.

"Bullshit." said Rob as he entered the conversation. He continued, "You are truly off in your own world, kid."

Jordan thought back again over when he had an opportunity to help. There was certainly Bill's drug smuggling, but that wasn't fair, that wasn't making the world a better place. Then there was Ali's shop, it was a wonder Ali even kept him around. He spent so little time there and was such a flake. Why was no one coming up to him asking for help?

"Maybe you spend all your time asking for help and never have the time to help others."

"How can I help you, Hans?" Jordan responded.

"You're going to take over driving when we get out of town." Hans responded.

CHAPTER THIRTY

THE TRIO MADE GOOD TIME to London and pulled up in front of the address Rob had written down just after eleven that evening. 77 Jacob Street, in SE1. The building looked modern, recently built or renovated, primarily concrete on the outside with some neon green panels that gave it a hip and trendy appearance. The street was quiet, mostly office spaces with a few residential buildings sandwiched between them.

Jordan sat and waited for Rob or Hans to exit the car before he did, hoping to get some assurance he wasn't going this alone before setting out. A few awkward minutes passed with no one leaving the car, finally he spoke up.

"Staying in the car then?" he asked, hopeful he might persuade them to join him.

"This is your part, Jordan. Good luck." Hans said with a surprisingly solemn tone.

Jordan looked out the window and up at the building that may or may not contain his mother. He saw a few of the windows lit up from inside, blinds closed. It was quite possible the woman with his mother's name who resided here was of no relation to him, but his heart was nonetheless filled with butterflies, snakes and jellyfish. He thought back to the dream that inspired him to end up at this doorstep. The feeling of overwhelming love and joy he had experienced echoed in his mind but he couldn't recreate it at this moment. What laid inside? Who? And if it was her, how would she react?

This was an awful time to show up, she was probably asleep, maybe waiting until tomorrow would be better, more appropriate, he thought. Or perhaps he should just send a letter tomorrow with his contact info and stay in town to see if she responds.

Then Jordan thought about his lack of a computer or cell phone, what address or phone number would he give her? Electric-powered communication technology would have been useful in this situation, Jordan admitted to himself. But he still detested it, and realized this very moment was a perfect example of how technologies enable detachment, impersonal and indirect communication. Technology would not have benefitted him here, it would have hindered him, it was a diversion.

Taking a deep inhalation of the rather dirty city air, Jordan held his breath and opened the car door. Afraid he might turn back, he jumped out of the station wagon and ran up to the building entrance.

There were a surprising number of names on the call box for such a small building. Half-way down, the label read "Santarelli." Jordan pushed the adjacent call button without giving himself time to think.

A dull, perforated tone played through the speaker on the call box and Jordan stood in anticipation, considering that he still had the option to run off and not say a word.

He also considered that there may be no answer to run away from. After the fifth ring, a click sounded and a woman's voice answered, "'Ello?"

"Um, yes, uh, this is Jordan. Your s-s-son?" Jordan's hesitant response was more of a question than a statement.

The box made another clicking noise and then went silent. Jordan reached to pull the entrance door open, but it remained locked.

"Hello?" he asked.

There was no response. Jordan took a final look through the obscured glass between the call box and the front door, but only saw the blackness of the unlit foyer. Had they really traveled fourteen hours for this? For a click of a call box? What lunacy.

Jordan turned and walked toward the car. As he reached for the passenger seat, he heard the building's front door unlatch and the same voice he heard over the call box screeched out, "Jordan!"

Turning, he saw a woman leaning out the entrance with one foot on the pavement. Illuminated by the light hanging above the door, Jordan saw her hair, long and devoid of pigment, petite glasses perched on her nose and wrinkled skin with a staunch frown completed the rather wicked expression on her face.

Jordan approached the building entrance and took a closer look at the woman, comparing her to the images in his memory. Was this her? Was this his mother?

"Come inside, it's cold out here." She instructed him, holding the door open as she stepped back into the building.

He followed her in with a mix of joy and confusion,

still uncertain if this was his mother or just a lonely old woman.

When they arrived at her flat and she opened the door, Jordan saw how they fit so many names on the call box. The apartment was tiny, slightly more than a single room, only because of the open door that revealed a small bathroom in the far corner next to the wall that faced the entrance and held only a single, disproportionately small, window. The room reeked of cigarette smoke and Jordan saw the muted television blasting various arrangements and color upon the well-worn recliner sitting opposite. A small, double sized bed lay next to the window against the far wall.

"Tea?" asked the woman.

"You are Jane Santarelli, right?"

"Don't recognize me then? Hardly surprising, it's been over a decade. But I remember you Jordan, I haven't forgotten you." She pointed to a 5x7 framed high school graduation portrait with Jordan's smiling face that stood on the counter next to the water boiler.

Jordan's head raced with questions while his heart beat with the joyful pleasure of reuniting with his mother and completing his journey. This was her, his mother, alive, living in London of all places. Her flat lacked the homeliness he had given it in his imagination, just as his mother lacked the joy and welcome he was expecting. It was unclear if she was happy or upset at his arrival. Her lack of emotion made it impossible for him to respond with any of the joy, sorrow, love and curiosity that began to soak into his mind.

As Jane prepared tea for two, Jordan walked in a

small circle, taking in the apartment, searching to see if he had missed anything in his initial inventory of the humble abode.

"Take a seat, hon. Tell me what brought you here. Or rather, how did you even find me?"

Jordan paused. He was irritated with her nonchalant attitude. "You, mother. You brought me here. I journeyed half way around the world, after not seeing you since I was a teenager and by some miraculous stroke of luck managed to find you. Do you have any idea how much I sacrificed to be here?"

"Calm down, my son. Why are you so angry?"

Jordan began to wonder the same thing, how did a mission fueled by love come into fruition with such resentment? He took a deep breath in and looked back up at his mother. "I'm sorry. I just. I thought. I can't believe it's you." he finally said.

Jane remained silent. Jordan thought about what was happening and compared it with what he had expected to happen. Where was the warm greeting? Not even a hug or a kiss for her long lost son? Refusing to accept such a disappointing family reunion, Jordan jumped up from the recliner and walked up to his mother with a hug, finally saying what was in his heart: "I missed you."

His mother returned the embrace and kissed him on the cheek, then responded to Jordan's admission in kind, as the ice that had built up between the two and led to such a hostile encounter finally burst into water. For the first time since having that dream on the dock, Jordan felt his heart warm with the love that had been so absent for most of his life.

As the two pulled apart, Jordan saw tears running down his mother's face. She looked up at him and with a hesitant, humble voice said "I did look for you. I just, I lost track of you."

"I was in a dark place, mum. It's probably for the best you didn't find me."

"How did you...how did you find me?" she asked, handing Jordan a cup of tea.

"A friend with some tech skills looked you up, it was a long shot."

Jane nodded, sighed and remarked "I suppose privacy is a thing of the past these days."

Jordan thought of all the questions he wanted to ask his mother now that the quest he thought was impossible had been completed. Since beginning his search, he had spent little time thinking about what he would say or do if he ever actually found her. Unsure what to say, he stopped thinking and took a moment to simply enjoy the warmth in his heart.

Taking their tea out of the nook of a kitchen, the two made due with the only available seating: Jane sat on the bed facing Jordan in the recliner turned toward her. The two spent hours recounting their life stories since they had parted ways. Jordan skipped over the dark parts, which didn't leave him with much to say. But he did mention his failed attempts to bring down the grid in Seattle.

Jane had a rather short, depressing story, or at least that is what she shared with Jordan. After spending three years living out of a backpack, traveling around Europe by rail and sleeping in tents or on strangers' couches, she settled into London where she married a bartender, primarily making their relationship official to aid Jane in obtaining citizenship.

The fellow's name was Damien. But a few months after their courtroom wedding, another woman caught his eye. Legally, Jane was still married to him, but they stopped living together years ago and he has gone off to do his own thing, never settling down.

After nearly a decade bagging groceries, Jane hit retirement age and was now receiving her sole income from the government. She lived modestly and spent most of her days watching TV, reading books and participating in the social circle she had found at the pub where she met Damien.

"Was it worth it? Leaving behind everyone to escape from America?"

"Think of what I would be doing now if I hadn't, Jordan. Probably continuing to bag groceries for even less than I made here, living off the pennies that Social Security provided me, eating cat food and barely able to pay rent. Of course I'm glad I left. But you, you're young, I can see why leaving home wasn't as appealing to you."

Perhaps he should have gone with her Jordan thought. Maybe he would have been happier living over here and never gotten into trouble with C.L. and Bill. At the time when she was leaving, something in Jordan's conscious told him she didn't want him to come with her. He felt abandoned at the time, but now he saw that his abandonment was his own doing. He could have gone with her.

"I wanted to stay. I thought if I refused to go, you would stay too. When you left anyways, I was heartbroken and felt abandoned." The honest admission lifted a tremendous weight from Jordan's shoulders that had been pushing him down since she had left.

"You're just as stubborn as I am, Jordan." Jane responded with a laugh. "Now, tell me what you're new plan is to save the world, since those escapades in Seattle fizzled out. What are you going to do, my superhero son?"

As the question came from Jane's mouth, images of Hannah flooded Jordan's imagination. The art supplies she had given him while he was in prison, the way she had turned the coffee shop into a warm, welcoming place with her painting and fresh flowers. He had resisted her solution for so long, but after trying every alternative he could think of he was ready to admit defeat. Her solution was now his solution as well. Making his small dent in the universe would be done by spreading love through art, and it would not be a quick fix, it would take time. It would take his entire lifetime.

Returning to the present moment, he responded simply, "With art. And with love."

He went on to share his first artistic endeavors and learned about the few unfulfilled sparks of creative inspiration Jane had in her younger years. The two continued talking about their ideas for art projects until the early hours of the morning, the sun began to rise and its beams illuminated the room.

Seeing the rays of light shining through, Jordan thought of Rob and Hans in the car outside. "What time is it? I better check on my friends." he remarked, getting up to see if they were still waiting for him.

"Oh my, it's way past my bedtime." Jane responded,

shaking her head and looking at her wristwatch. "Nearly six already!"

Jordan walked down to the building's entrance and peered out the front door, where he saw Hans' car still parked on the street. The two men appeared to be sleeping inside.

Returning to his mother's flat, he told her they must continue catching up this afternoon, once she had gotten some rest. He himself was so inspired, excited and hopeful after their encounter the thought of sleep was the furthest thing from his mind. After making plans to meet at a nearby cafe in the afternoon, Jordan said goodbye to his mother and returned to the car. Finding that his door was still unlocked, he slid in and sat silently waiting for his companions to wake up. Thoughts raced through his mind a mile per second and one particular idea began to take shape: He must find a way to stay in Europe and be with his mother.

CHAPTER THIRTY-ONE

A FTER ABOUT HALF AN HOUR of sitting quietly in the car, Jordan could no longer wait for Hans and Rob to wake up. He figured Hans would be the least upset if woken up, so he nudged his shoulder a few times until Hans awoke from his slumber.

Disoriented and in a bit of a haze, Hans took his bearings and turned his gaze to Jordan in the seat behind him. Hans was groggy and surprised by the light outside and chill in the car, he opened his mouth a few times before he began to speak.

"I must have fallen asleep. How long were you up there?"

"A while, I was worried you wouldn't be out here. It was her, Hans! My mother! Can you believe it?"

"Of course it was! I knew you would find her! The family reunited at last, how about that?"

"We talked all night, she seems happy here. Tiny flat, but she gets by."

"So now what?"

"I want to stay here, Hans. I have to."

"Live with your mum then?"

"No, no. That's not what I meant. Stay here in London.

I'll get a job, find a place to live. I must! I finally have family, Hans!"

Jordan sounded half maniacal, crazed with his newfound desire to hang on to the feeling of love that had finally reignited in his heart upon reuniting with his mother. As he sat in the car and considered how he could make it work here, he could already feel the warmth in his heart beginning to fade. He couldn't wait to see his mother that afternoon and tell her his new plan.

He knew Hans would support him, and perhaps Rob could help him with the legal issues involved. Jordan counted on their support, his dream was fragile now, he didn't know if he could stand any criticism at this point.

Hans took some time before responding, but finally provided the encouragement that Jordan had been waiting for and suggested they visit the immigration office once Rob woke up.

"I'm up. I've been up since you two started talking." Rob announced, emerging from his false hibernation. "We're not doing anything before we eat breakfast though. I'm starving and it's too early for any government office to be open anyway."

The trio left the car where it had been parked all night and departed on foot to venture into the city in search of bacon and eggs. As they crossed over the River Thames on a foot bridge the city presented itself en masse for the first time. Jordan had never seen anything like it, he stopped mid-step, gawking at the magnificence of London. The Tower of London stood directly in front of them, its ancient stone structure emitting a foreboding reminder of the history that they were walking through.

On the other side of the river, the sidewalk grew crowded and the roads were filled with cars, black taxis and bright red double-decker busses taking people on their morning commute. Wandering the streets in hopes of finding a nice diner, they finally settled into a cafe they passed by after about five blocks of directionless exploration.

As they dined on fresh smoked bacon, perfectly cooked eggs and strong coffee, Jordan recounted his evening to Rob and Hans. They listened with interest and voiced their support and happiness at his accomplishment and he bolstered up the courage to share his new plan with Rob that he had divulged to Hans earlier.

"I want to stay. I'm going to stay."

"It's bloody expensive to live here, kid. You think Seattle is bad, hah." Rob responded dismissively.

"But there are poor people here, just like in Seattle. Surely it's not impossible for all income brackets to live here. Where do those with less live? I've never seen a city successfully extinguish the poor. After all, who would refill the city dwellers' coffee cups if that were to happen?"

"Sure, you can live outside the city. Maybe get by. But why go to that trouble?"

"To be near my mother, of course. What made you so justified in your move to Copenhagen?"

"Not the same thing, Jordan. I had money saved up, plenty of it. The NSA pays employees quite well to keep their secrets. And I knew that moving out here was the only way I could leave the agency before retirement."

"So you were on the run. You're right, it's not the same

thing. I'm saying I want to stay here to be with my mother. What better reason could there be?"

"Then what when she dies?"

"Can you ever be positive, Rob? C'mon man!" Hans interjected. "He just reunited with his mother after a decade and you want to talk about when she dies?" Hans slapped Rob on the back, half jovially and half violently.

"Fine, fine." Rob surrendered.

The three finished dining and went on an improvised self-guided walking tour of the city. The beauty and authority of each passing street, building, and person reinforced Jordan's desire to stay here. Every structure in the city spoke a different dialect than the cardboard cut-outs of Seattle. Nothing here was disposable, nothing was soon to be torn down without careful consideration, and even then only with the assurance that whatever took its place would be even more magnificent. It was overwhelming, the city was a work of art that stretched for miles. A living and breathing act of creation that was the result of hundreds of years of devoted labor and civilization.

As they approached Hyde Park, Jordan ran into the grassy expanse and laid down on his back. He pressed his back against the earth and stared up into the heavens while declaring this city his own. Breathing deeply, he attempted to merge his spirit with this place, to become one and carry it forward by contributing his life's energy to its continued growth as the height of human civilization.

Hans and Rob looked down at Jordan as if he were a child.

"It's mine! Mine! This city."

"You like it, eh? If you think this is good you should see Paris." Hans responded with a grin.

"Let's go to immigration!" Jordan shouted as he rose up from the grass and stared excitedly at Hans.

"Alright, alright. What's the harm?"

Rob pulled up directions on his phablet and led the group through the park toward a nearby government building. Inside, they confronted a wall of paperwork and a queue. After an hour's wait, Jordan was called forward and approached the counter, the fear of his fantasy becoming a reality emerging as sweat greased his palms and hesitation pounded through his head.

"I'm visiting, and I want to stay." Jordan informed the clerk.

"Oh, well let me go print you off a passport then. Be back in a flash." The clerk responded mockingly with a frown from the chair she remained seated in.

"Hah, right. Yeah, um. I mean, my mother lives here. She immigrated from America. I came to find her, and now that I have, I want to stay."

"Right then, well she needs to come here with you. And you'll need to fill out some forms, then we might be able to get you a temporary work visa."

The clerk handed Jordan a packet of stapled paperwork and dismissed him, calling for the next person in the queue.

Jordan thought over what had happened over the past twenty-four hours. Reflecting on the day-long drive across Europe, when he didn't know if he would even find his mother, to standing in the immigration office after having been reunited with his mother and hopeful to move to England himself. Maybe he really was crazy.

"So? What'd she say?" Hans asked as Jordan returned to the two who had been seated waiting on him.

"She gave me some paperwork, gotta bring my mother back here she said. But there's a chance, at least for a temporary visa."

Rob's eyebrows raised, revealing his surprise. "So you're going to join us here in Europe, eh?" He asked, attempting to mask his doubt of the prospect even being possible.

"When are you meeting with your mother next?"

Jordan looked up at a large clock on the wall and saw he only had an hour before he would see her. "Soon, gotta find our way to Hampstead."

"We'll take the tube for that." Hans responded.

"Maybe he doesn't want us along, Hans." Rob questioned.

"You guys have been so kind, I owe you the world. But I don't want to keep you here in London. You probably want to get back to Denmark."

"You're really going to stay, are you? Where will you sleep tonight?"

"I'll figure it out, don't worry about me."

"What about your friends back home? And your job?" Hans broke in. "I thought you were joking. You don't actually think you can just up and start living here, do you? No visa, no money." Hans looked distressed.

Jordan frowned, his precious idea just lost its chief cheerleader. But at this point the spark had ignited into a flame in his heart and he was determined not to rely on

Hans or anyone else to be his soul's kindler. He could be his own advocate.

"I'll figure it out. Don't worry about me." Jordan repeated.

Rob jotted down some information on a piece of paper and handed it to Jordan. Reading it, Jordan took note of the phone numbers and address back in Copenhagen. He nodded with relief that he was finally being taken seriously, but at the same time was deeply terrified that he now had to live out the idea that had seemed so grand in his imagination. Only the thought of his mother and having love in his heart kept him from shattering into a million pieces.

"Well, the tube station is just down that way. You can use the map in the station to find your way to Hampstead. I guess this is goodbye." Hans said somberly, his traditional upbeat enthusiasm lacking.

"I'll visit you guys. Once I'm settled in here. I can't thank you enough, I would never have found her without you."

Rob and Hans each gave Jordan a parting hug and then went on their way back to the car by foot.

Jordan took the tube to Hampstead and found the cafe he was to meet his mother at. He was a bit early and ordered a coffee as he sat at an open table and thought over what he would say when she arrived.

It was half past when she finally showed up, Jordan had been nearly ready to give up and leave if it wasn't for the fact that he had nowhere else to go. Seeing his mother in the bright light of the cafe, Jordan took in a new image of her, with details that were lacking in the dim light of her flat. He noticed her weary face and hesitant step assisted by a cane as she walked toward his table leaning forward in a hunch and walking with a limp.

After helping her take a seat, Jordan asked if she wanted a coffee and was perturbed by her refusal.

The two finished pleasantries and then Jordan couldn't hold back his excitement any longer, "Mother, I'm going to move here to London! I've decided it and already met with immigration. I want to have a family again."

Jane was shocked, she leaned back in her chair and tilted her head down to look at Jordan above her reading glasses. After extending the pause for a few moments more, she finally responded, "No."

It was the last response Jordan expected from her. Why was she not overjoyed? This was not going as planned. Why was she being so difficult?

"What?" he responded with exasperation.

"You need to save the world, Jordan. I heard your inspiration last night, that's what you need to follow."

"But. I can do that here. It's family, that's what is the most important."

"America needs people like you more than England does, my love. I feel your pain, I've felt it my entire life, it's what brought me out here. And when I arrived I found the society I was looking for. It's not perfect here, there's still corruption, pollution and I'm certainly not rich or living a life of luxury. But it's the culture that fits me. and I'm better taken care of than I would be back home. People care about each other here, government serves the people and it's a majestic city to live in."

"Yes, exactly! It's just what I need."

"No, it's not. It's what you want. What you need is to go back and save our homeland. If everyone who craves progress flees America, then the corrupt and greedy powers will concentrate and turn their eyes toward expanding abroad. America is not a terrorist sect, but its sick corporate culture of ever expanding power and oppression creates a threat to the peace we enjoy here. It's a society built on hate and selfishness, but it can change. Things were not so good here until quite recently when you look at the long history."

"But. Don't you. Don't you want family? Can't family transcend the evil? Fuck the American culture of greed, I can't save them from themselves."

"We can use technology, son. You can help fix America and you can have family. I don't want to lose touch with you again. Just setup Skype for me before you leave and we can talk every day until you're absolutely sick of me if you like."

"Why me? I would rather be rid of that culture than change it. I can stay here and be happy."

"Then what's your life for? What's your legacy? You retreated into the woods and died. Is that it?"

Jordan paused, looking up at the ceiling he reflected on his mother's words rather than lashing back with another response. Was she right? Did he really need to go back home despite finding a utopia here in Europe? Why? He had tried to fight the culture of mindless consumption in America and it blew up in his face, quite literally. He knew that art and compassion had the power to make positive change, but it was slow and a transformation that would take generations. Why fight that fight when there was refuge here in Europe where victory had already been won over the greedy and corrupt?

Jane continued, "You will regret it if you stay, trust me. I have regretted my decision at times, but now I have no option but to stay, there is nothing for me if I return home. I'm taken care of here. I'm too old and worn to resume working, a life of manual labor wears you down, Jordan. I hope you find something better, with your art. You have so much ahead of you. If you come here what will you do? What will inspire your art?"

Jordan's heart sank into his chest, he ached as if he had just suffered a punch to the gut. He knew she was right, but he still hated it. He liked to think that he could find victory in his own lifetime, not have to devote his entire life just to be a part of victory that probably wouldn't take place until long after his death. Where was the glory in that? There was none. He took a deep breath in and exhaled slowly. None of this changed the fact that she was right, she spoke the truth and it was undeniable.

"I was hoping you would want me to stay. I thought I could make you happy here."

"I'm the only one who can make me happy, Jordan. I learned that, it took a few repeat lessons, but I know it with absolute certainty now. Having you in my life does bring me joy, but you don't need to sacrifice your life to make me happy. That's good news, isn't it?"

"You don't seem that happy to me." Jordan said, being genuinely honest about his impression of her for the first time.

"I have a mind full of regret. I'll tell you what. You want to make me happy? Carry on my legacy. Take the hard road, fight the good fight and help fix our broken country. Then I can die knowing that at least I made something good in my life."

Jordan stared into his mother's eyes and saw a twinkle of hope suddenly emerge in what had previously been a dark and dreary gaze. A spark of life returned to her expression and took away the misery that had previously been dominant. There was no denying that America needed him more than England did, and he admitted to himself that he surely didn't want to end up being the bundle of regret that he saw in front of him when he grew old.

"You can make art and spread love too, you know? There are still ways you can help make the world a better place. Write a song, help another elderly person, do something."

"I do, Jordan. You assume the worst in me, you know? I have friends, I have a life here. I sing and dance believe it or not. I'm okay. You worry about me worrying about you but it sounds like you're mostly just worried about me. I'm fine. You don't need to worry anymore."

"So I'll go back then. Home." Jordan said, more to himself than to his mother. The truth of his journey's conclusion sinking in.

CHAPTER THIRTY-TWO

THE TWO PARTED WAYS AFTER exchanging contact information and Jordan setting up Skype on his mother's phone. He promised to call as soon as he was back in Seattle. After leaving the cafe, he took a little bit of time to wander Hampstead and take in as much of London as he could before making his way to the airport.

Changing his ticket was a bit complicated and required several repeated attempts, speaking with different airline representatives, before they finally showed him a bit of mercy and got him on a flight departing later that evening, with a connection through Atlanta. It would be a long journey, and the more Jordan thought about leaving the less he wanted to.

He felt safe here in Europe, he had made friends over the course of his brief visit, reunited with his mother, discovered beautiful cities and most importantly found a society that looked out for the greater good. It was a paradise. He didn't even know such a place existed before his arrival, and now that he had found it he couldn't see how returning home to Seattle made any sense. He had to acknowledge his own selfish nature before he could face the more painful truth that required him to return to America. It was scary, terrifying really, to imagine the amount of work that was needed to make even a small change in such a sick and suffering society.

One drawing at a time, one kind word or act at a time, one day at a time, for the rest of his life. Accepting the reality that he may not see the triumph of the social revolution he would devote his life toward was a cause for concern, not just because it would take away his sense of victory, but because it meant he would never know for certain if the battle was won. Some sort of afterlife where he could look out upon the living world was his only hope for seeing what would happen.

Maybe up there, in the heavens or whatever afterlife might exist, there was already a chorus of others who have worked for progress eagerly watching him and his compatriots, cheering them on. He only need tap into that spiritual energy and he could drive himself forward with faith that his devotion to bringing the world a step further was worthwhile.

Jordan sat staring out at the airplanes taking off and landing while he waited for his flight. He couldn't help but consider the carbon they were all spewing into the atmosphere, including the jet he would soon ride half way around the planet. Everything was clotting up the atmosphere, the lights throughout the concourse, the machines that built the chair he sat on, the factory that made the clothes he was wearing. It seemed impossible to live without adding to the destruction. Jordan only hoped that he might balance it out by minimizing what he consumed and expelling as much of his life energy toward a better future as possible.

His thoughts returned to Hannah, Ali and William. His hope, his inspiration. He counted on them being there for him when he returned. For a job, a place to stay and inspiration to keep going with his newfound artistic endeavor. The drawing supplies Hannah had given him returned to his mind and he pulled them out from his bag.

As he continued watching the jets make their way, people entering and exiting through the gateways, Jordan began drawing a canoe. He thought of the Native Americans who dwelled in his homeland and lived in harmony with nature long before any of his white-skinned ancestors had arrived. He thought of how the natives found a balance, using the fruits of the world around them to sustain and enjoy their lives, while never crossing the line and doing more harm to the environment than good. This was how he wanted to live, and even with as much drive as he had to live according to his beliefs in a sustainable way, his thoughts immediately turned to toilets, showers, running water, heaters and electric light bulbs. He liked these things, he didn't want to lose these things.

The fact that people lived for thousands of years without such basic amenities was difficult for him to accept. Was modernity a forbidden fruit? Surely if the Germanic tribes had been given toilets early on, they would have never gone back to their traditional ways. Where was the balance? Could we make and use toilets without destroying our environment?

Jordan's mind shifted to China. Hundreds of thousands, perhaps millions of Chinese humans working in factories so large they were beyond the grasp of his American imagination. Making the toilets. Making the smartphones. Making absolutely everything the American dollar could buy. He wondered if one day we might outsource our mint to China, wouldn't that be great? American dollars, made in China.

Those workers, those souls, they were human, there was no denying that. The magnificent robotic manufacturing dream had never been accomplished. Instead we had what some might call slavery on a grander scale than at any previous point in history. Eleven Chinese humans to a bunk room, with barely enough space in the room to get in and out of their beds. Not enough money to live somewhere nicer. The forty hour work week was a dream for them, they worked sixty, sometimes eighty hours per week to churn out the gadgets that the rest of the world had to get their hands on.

How could we buy products knowing they were made in such awful conditions, by such mistreated workers? Perhaps the same way we ate food picked by migrants who were beaten and paid rotten wages on American farms. Slavery was not over with the civil war. No, we had simply evolved slavery in the modern manufacturing world by creating "free trade" and "globalization." These words sounded so liberating, so progressive on the surface.

How far had we fallen from virtue? After all, didn't we, the white Christian folk, once live like "savage" natives? Where had we gone wrong? When did we lose our hearts?

As Jordan became overwhelmed with despair, hardly knowing how this one little sketch of a canoe he had made would help make anything better, he spotted a child, a young girl not more than three years old, light blonde hair bouncing in the air as she ran around the waiting area. She was full of joy, pleasure, innocence, not knowing all of the tragedies that surrounded here.

The girl stood on the chair next to her mother, a few empty seats down the bench from where Jordan sat, and looked back at Jordan. She had a beaming smile and bright blue eyes open wide as she stared at him. She reached out her hand as if making a peace offering.

Jordan was petrified, never knowing how to act around children, he waved his hand at the child and forced a smile onto his face.

The girl slowly took a few steps across the row of chairs toward Jordan, arm remaining outstretched, grin only expanding as she grew nearer. Her wide-eyed stare remained transfixed on Jordan, and Jordan was in awe of the child's glowing aura.

Doubt, despair and misery vanished instantaneously from his mind. As he looked at the girl he felt nothing but hope, his heart filled with love and inspiration. He had a chance to prove to this child that there was reason to smile, despite all the awful things going on. At the same time, the child's innocence and love gave him the motivation and perspective to see the good that still existed in the world around him, left behind only because of the hard work of the people who had fought for justice before him.

Jordan took a deep breath, said a prayer of gratitude and finished his drawing.

ABOUT THE AUTHOR

Philip Palios was born in 1985 and has lived in the Seattle area for most of his life.

www.philthycreative.com

ACKNOWLEDGEMENTS

First and foremost, my deepest gratitude goes to you, reader of independent literature, for stepping outside the bounds of the publishing establishment and giving this book a chance.

I'm quite grateful for my mentors who introduced me to literature and inspired my creative and philosophical aspirations: Jeffery White, Russ Payne, Geraldine Grimm, William Baldwin and Fred Turner. I also owe special thanks to Edan Lepucki for teaching me that the only thing standing between me and my first novel was a blank page.

I never would have finished writing this novel if it wasn't for the ceaseless encouragement and excitement from my friends and family. Especially my mother, for her challenging questions and help coming up with a tagline.

Cherry Street Coffee in Seattle and Roost Coffee in Pullman provided me with the essential ingredients for the countless hours I spent working on this novel: excellent coffee and a pleasant writing environment.

Finally, I thank Glendon Haddix and Streetlight Graphics for their brilliant cover design and interior formatting.

Made in the USA
San Bernardino, CA
08 January 2017